Robert Westall

Break
of
Dark

RED FOX DEFiniTiOnS

BREAK OF DARK

A RED FOX BOOK: 0099439530

First published in Great Britain by Chatto & Windus Ltd
Chatto & Windus Ltd edition published 1932
The Bodley Head edition published 1984
Red Fox edition published 2003

1 3 5 7 9 10 8 6 4 2

Copyright © Robert Westall, 1982

Printed and bound in Great Britain by Clays Ltd, St Ives PLC

Set in Adobe Garamond
Red Fox Books are published by Random House Children's Books,
61–63 Uxbridge Road, London W5 5SA,

The Random House Group Limited supports The Forest Stewardship
Council (FSC®), the leading international forest certification organisation.
Our books carrying the FSC label are printed on FSC® certified paper.
FSC is the only forest certification scheme endorsed by the leading
environmental organisations, including Greenpeace. Our
paper procurement policy can be found at
www.randomhouse.co.uk/environment

THE RANDOM HOUSE GROUP Limited Reg. No. 954009

www.kidsatrandomhouse.co.uk

A CIP catalogue record for this book is available from the British Library.

Addresses for companies within The Random House Group Limited
can be found at: www.randomhouse.co.uk/offices.htm

For my friend Bob Megraw
late navigator, Bomber Command,
and Careers Officer extraordinary

Contents

HITCH-HIKER

It is more than ten years now since I went climbing in the Red Cuillins on the Isle of Skye, leaving behind me a broken engagement and a broken heart. Sylvia had fallen for one of our college lecturers, a divorcé with a lot of money, his own house and roving hands. He was nearly twice my age; there's not much a twenty-year-old can do against that kind of opposition.

In a careless, cheerful way, I didn't care whether I lived or died. I climbed like a maniac, I climbed like a genius. The red gabbro rock of the Cuillin grips your boots like sandpaper; you feel you can climb up a vertical wall like a fly. The July sun was warm on my back, through only a thin, worn shirt. I felt invincible. But if I wasn't, then there'd just be a long flight through space, and I wouldn't have to think about Sylvia any more when I first wakened up in the morning. That's all I thought there was: glorious life or sudden death. Like the song said, that we used to sing in the evenings:

They scraped him off Great Gable like a pound of
    strawberry jam
And he ain't going to climb no more.

The thought of being a paraplegic, a cabbage in a wheelchair, a prisoner for the rest of my life, just hadn't occurred to me.

David and Harry should have steadied me; Harry was a cheerful little lad, a game climber who didn't give a thought to his occasional attacks of asthma. David was slow and funny, and always seemed to have time for everything and everybody. Well, he always had time for me. But my madness seemed to infect them. We came down Sgurr a Greadaigh by a gully full of rotten stone that must never have been climbed in the history of Skye; a gully that no mountaineer in his right mind would go near. Seemed like half the mountain was following us down in lumps as big as hens -- and us crouching on a narrow ledge as they burst around us like an artillery bombardment, laughing our little heads off.

We walked away without a scratch.

We jumped the Mauvais Pas on Sgurr Alasdair, whooping like cowboys; came down by the Stone-chute that hadn't been worn out in those days and was just like ski-ing. In short, we had a ball for ten whole days. Even the ferocious Skye midges, forcing their way into the tents in the evening against a barrage of fag-smoke and eating away avidly at the open jar of insect-repellent, were a giggle.

Then the August rains set in, and it all went sour. Harry's asthma came on with a vengeance. We hurried him across to the mainland as fast as we could, and then tried to hitch-hike home to Geordyland. But who wants three soaking-wet hitch-hikers with big knobbly boots and framed rucksacks that could scratch the enamel off your car at any moment? We waited together half a day, then decided to split up. Two together might make it; three never would. – and David had the big, non-leaky tent, and was much more patient with somebody sick than I was. So I walked off down the road and left them to it. Ten minutes later they passed me, waving wildly, perched among sacks of stinking fishmeal on the back of a lorry marked GLASGOW. I never saw them again; I hope they've had happy lives. They were good mates.

Me, I had a high old time. Went down Glen Shiel on the back of a motorbike in a thunderstorm. Went down Glen Alby behind the luggage in the back of a van, while the family prattled cheerfully about their holidays and I had to be sick into my sandwich box out of politeness, and they never even noticed or shut up for a minute. They dropped me on the northern outskirts of Fort William. A weak sun came out; I felt purged and cheerful. I had done the hard bit. I still had five pounds in my wallet and I could coast home as gently as I wished, stopping and staring whenever I felt inclined. In a fit of euphoria, I cleaned out my rucksack and dumped the remains of my grub: a stale half-loaf, a bag of over-ripe plums and a packet of butter that had melted in the sun five times. I dumped them and the sandwich box (friend of the countryside that I was) under some very prickly brambles in a rather wet ditch. Then I walked into Fort William and treated myself to the loo in the railway station.

Unfortunately, as I was sitting thinking in solitary state, my trousers round my ankles and my wallet sticking half out of my back pocket, a crafty Fort William hand came under the wooden partition and helped itself to my wallet. I remember the hand was pale, freckled and had little ginger hairs all over it. But by the time I'd pulled myself together and got my trousers up, the freckled hand had turned into a set of rapidly retreating footsteps that soon mingled with the holiday crowds outside. I walked about for an hour looking for that hand; but most people had their hands in their trouser-pockets anyway.

I didn't bother to go to the police station. Instead, I walked back to the northern outskirts and retrieved my half-loaf, butter and rotten plums from the very prickly ditch. Contact with muddy water had not improved them. Then I set about getting home as quickly as possible, before I starved to death. Scottish hospitality had left me with twenty-two pence in my pocket. I got a ride on a mass of empty milk-churns as far as Ardlui, at the northern end of Loch Lomond, and then my luck ran out. For hitch-hiking, the Lomond road is a bastard, however lovely the scenery. You see, the bonny, bonny banks of the said loch zig-zag in and out, and the Lomond road zig-zags with them, every forty yards. And the one thing a hitch-hiker must do is to stand where a car can see him a hundred yards away, to give the driver time to pull up. I walked fourteen miles looking for that hundred-yard straight, and never found it. And it rained a lot, and the more it rains, the less likely you are to get a hitch.

So by nine in the evening, very footsore and sorry for myself, I was near the southern end of the loch, just north of Balloch. There, there are caravan sites between the road and the loch, and on the other side of the road, a steep, wild and magnificent hillside of bracken ascends halfway to the sky. Fine to camp, if you can find a flat six feet to take your tent, and if you watch where you're putting your feet; they never seem to provide enough toilets on those caravan sites, and there's a lot of do-it-yourself among the bracken. *And* courting couples; the Scots have some funny tastes. Still, the Scottish Tourist Board laid on a magnificent sunset for me, and the loch looked just like all the songs and poems said. And I sat at the door of my tent like Abu Ben Adem, eating soggy bread and rotten plums and smelling the hamburgers frying in the caravan park.

I became aware eventually, even through the choking clouds of self-pity, that there was a persistent rustling in the bracken behind my tent. Ho, I thought, what Scottish goody is this? A cow, to trample my tent flat? Or the Dr Moriarty of Fort William station loo come back for my trousers? I leapt up with the ferocity of a tiger and flung myself in the general direction of the noise, tripping over a guy-rope in the process. The noise rapidly retreated before me, as I plunged deeper and deeper into the head-high bracken. I was just starting to wonder if someone was luring me away while his mate stole my tent, when the something stopped and stood still. I could just see a bit of it through the bracken. It had two legs and was very pale. I lunged, and stopped, my mouth gaping.

A girl was standing there, stark naked, her arms crossed across her breasts, looking at me with exactly the air of a startled deer. God, she was a smasher. Long silky blonde hair, long shapely legs, slightly cut and bleeding in one place from the bracken stems. Even with her arms crossed where they were, I could see that *Men Only* had nothing on her. It was, I suppose, every adolescent's wish-fulfilment. Except she was blue and goose-fleshed with cold, and I couldn't help thinking that the braw Scot who'd coaxed her into this state was likely at any moment to manifest himself like a roaring lion seeking whom he might devour.

I blurted into my innocent-bystander routine. Her eyes watched me; huge blue eyes. But they weren't terrified, or even embarrassed. They had the cool, appraising look that a rock climber has, the moment before he spits on his hands and makes a start on the central buttress of Great Gable.

'Please help me,' she said. I could tell from her voice that she was as much a lady as the Queen of England.

'What d'you want?'

'I am cold,' she said, glancing around still wary as a deer, but not of me. I didn't blame her; some funny things used to go on round Balloch; it's only ten miles from the edge of Glasgow, and the gangs went drinking up there in summer. 'Take me to your tent.'

I bundled her into my tent quick, before some libidinous Jock clapped eyes on her. Then I sat outside and hissed at her through the canvas.

'Where the hell are your clothes?' A Scottish mob crashed through the bracken only twenty yards away, going up the hillside, intent on upping the fertility of the place, one way or the other. Fear for her made me angry.

'I have had them stolen.' Her voice was muffled, but

maddeningly calm. 'Can you lend me some of yours?' She didn't sound at all tearful or beseeching; more like she was asking the way to the town hall.

It seemed a good idea. 'There's some stuff in my rucksack,' I said.

'What is a rucksack?'

'That big canvas thing, with all the straps on it.'

There was a pause. Then, 'What is canvas?' she asked.

Oh God, surely nobody could be that ignorant . . . More Jocks were approaching . . . I closed my eyes and flung myself into the tent, and collided with a mass of warm, yielding curves. I grabbed blindly where I knew the rucksack should be, and only drew a deep, deep breath once I'd regained the fresh air again.

'Hurry up. I am cold.' *She* didn't seem the least put out by our recent collision.

What I had to offer her was not pretty. My camouflaged climbing trousers, caked with mud. A shirt stinking of a week's sweat. A thick pullover with darned elbows and a pair of filthy plimsolls. All crumpled to hell. *I* wouldn't have worn them again, before my mum had been at them. And I couldn't bring myself to offer socks or underwear. I stuffed the clothes back to her through the tent-flap as if I was stoking a hungry furnace.

The tent heaved for a bit, like two cats fighting in a sack, then she emerged, a bit red in the face, but quite composed. My stuff fitted her well enough; she was a big girl in every way; nearly six feet tall. I was surprised she didn't ask for the loan of a comb and mirror; but she used them once they were offered.

'That feller . . . who stole your clothes . . . he didn't *do* anything to you? I mean, I can call the police . . .'

You might think that for a guy who'd just been through a pretty torrid engagement, I was being a bit over-shy, wanting to call the police. I mean, one man, one woman, one tent. I was hardly outnumbered. But there was something . . . creepy about this girl. Her body was too perfect; so was her face. I mean, even the prettiest girls, even filmstars, have the odd spot or mole. Sylvia had faint blue veins showing on her thighs that I hadn't liked much. But this girl, not a blemish. Like a pin-up in a magazine, and they're made-up to hide their blemishes. And her voice: beautiful, ladylike, polite, formal. Like a female announcer on the telly. No *expression*. And not knowing what a rucksack was . . . I began to wonder if she'd escaped from the local loony-bin. *They* sometimes take off all their clothes and run about naked . . .

I looked up; her cool blue eyes were watching me.

'Don't worry,' she said. 'I will look after you. Have you something to eat? I have not eaten for some time. I think I am rather . . . hungry.'

I gave her the remains of the soggy loaf, smeared with thin oily butter. She demolished it without a grimace, as if it was a feast. I offered her the least rotten of the plums.

She swallowed them, stones and all.

I lay in the darkness, surreptitiously rolling over from side to side, to avoid waking her. I was wearing every stitch I had left, and I was *freezing*. She lay in my sleeping bag, facing me, fast asleep. A gentle zephyr came out of her mouth, lifted a lock of her golden hair, and warmed my face. I could have raped her or anything. As it was, I was lying there in a flat panic. What on earth was I to *do* with her? She'd told me her name was Joan Smith, which sounded as real as a three-pound note. Nobody had interfered with her, she said, apart from stealing her clothes. Beyond that, she'd told me nothing. *She* had asked all the questions. What was my name? Where was I going? Where was I a student? What did I study? It was like being interrogated by the Gestapo. After three hours nonstop, I was worn out, my mind in a whirl. But I still couldn't sleep. I was hungry as well as cold.

I turned over again, a bit too violently. She wakened.

'Why can you not sleep?'

'I'm hungry.' I didn't dare say I was cold, or she'd probably have me inside that sleeping bag with her, and then . . . I shivered.

'Why don't you eat some more food?'

'Haven't got any more.'

'Why?'

'I'm broke.'

'Where are you broken?' She reached an arm out of the sleeping bag and began to feel my legs, as if she thought they were injured. For the first time she showed a trace of anxiety. She obviously wanted me kept in good shape.

'Not *broken*. "Broke" means I have no money. Didn't you know that?'

'Broke,' she said thoughtfully. 'Broke.' As if she was committing some obscure fact to memory. Then, 'Come with me. Take me to the town. I can get you some money, quickly.'

She was out of the bag and into my camouflage trousers and pullover in a flash. Then she was out of the tent-flap and off down the bracken slope. I had to run hard to catch her; she could move. She kept on running when she hit the road and I had to pound in pursuit. She was obviously very fit; I'm no slouch myself, but I had a job keeping up with her. We reached the outskirts of Balloch in no time at all. What did she mean to do? Go on the game in after-midnight Balloch? Burgle a house?

She did neither. She made for the nearest pub and, stooping suddenly in the gutter outside the front door, held up something in the light of the solitary remaining street lamp. It was a fifty pence piece. She gave it to me. Then two ten pences, then three pennies. She'd trebled my capital in less than a minute. At least we could now afford breakfast.

'This is a good place to look,' she said. 'The men come out of the pub drunk and fumble for their bus fares home, and drop coins. We will find more at the bus stop.'

She did, too. Then she shinned over the back wall of the pub like an Olympic athlete, silent in plimsolls. When she returned, she pressed thirty-seven pence into my hand. 'When the drunken men go to relieve themselves,' she explained.

We spent the rest of the night in a fiscal tour of Balloch. She was incredible. She found two pound notes blowing about; she could smell money in the dark like a dog can smell a rabbit. All she would say is, 'It is the drunks. It is Friday night.' I'd forgotten that, with being climbing on the Isle of Skye.

We, or rather I, staggered back to the tent in the dawn. We were richer by six pounds, seventy-two pence. And I'd spent twenty pence on chocolate from a machine we'd found. She was still raring to go.

'You like money,' she said, head on one side thoughtfully, in a way I later got quite fond of.

'I like eating,' I said, biting into a chocolate bar and offering her one.

'This is quite pleasant,' she said. 'Better than your bread. But if you eat too much of it, it will harm your teeth.' She said it like a little girl repeating a lesson.

I, at least, slept with a full belly, and the renewed warmth of sunrise.

We ate chocolate again, packed up the gear and went back into Balloch about nine. There was a road sweeper, sweeping the gutter outside the pub. He looked a bit fed-up and was muttering to himself. I gathered he'd been hoping for some of the loot that was jingling in my pocket.

We had a real Scottish cooked breakfast in a café: porridge, bacon and egg, toast and home-made marmalade. The woman who served us gave Joan some funny looks, but she was obviously used to climbers beating a retreat from Skye.

'You'd better buy a bloody bra,' I said, ungraciously, for, revived by the breakfast, I was enjoying her every stretch and yawn.

'Yes,' she said, 'and pants and socks and a comb of my own – your hair is greasy. Give me four pounds.'

I begrudged it, but it was she who'd given it to me. 'Finish your meal,' she said. 'I shan't be long.'

She came back, announcing, 'I am much more comfortable now.' So was the waitress. But when I'd paid for the breakfast, we were down to almost our last pound again.

'Don't worry,' she said. 'I can get more money. I can get you all the money you want. I can make you a millionaire.'

I gave her a funny look, I remember, standing on the doorstep of that café. But she gave me a very straight look back, before I could begin to think she was some kind of nutcase again.

'Buy me a newspaper,' she said.

I spent a grudging four pence on a copy of the *Scotsman*. She dived straight to the back, to the racing pages, studied them with a tongue protruding from the corner of her full mouth, and announced, 'Put a pound on that horse. He will win. Twenty-five to one.'

'I will not,' I said. 'I want to eat . . .' I didn't hold with backing horses. My dad has always said it's a mug's game.

Her eyes grew fierce. 'Give me all the money that is mine.' For the first time, I was just a little scared of her.

I gave her eighty pence. 'Go ahead,' I said. 'Go ahead and lose it. Then you're on your own.'

'I will not lose it,' she said. 'Where is the betting-shop?'

There was only one betting-shop in Balloch then, and it

was decidedly scruffy, full of old men in caps and mufflers. But for a lady, she didn't bat an eyelid. Then we had to hang around waiting for the two-thirty race. It began to rain. We sat in the café, making cups of tea – paid for out of my last money – spin out as long as possible. At twenty-five past two, she left me. When she'd gone, I realized she hadn't even looked at my watch, which I always keep a quarter of an hour fast anyway. And there wasn't a clock in sight. And she certainly hadn't been wearing a watch of her own when I first saw her . . .

I waited, feeling bored and empty and pointless and cruel. I was going to enjoy walking out on her, when she came back empty-handed.

She came back carrying thirty-five pound notes. 'The odds lengthened,' she explained. She gave me a pound. 'Put that on Starway Boy in the three o'clock at Newton Abbot.' It sounded like an order. 'And drink some more tea. I am going shopping again. I like shopping.'

I won't draw out the whole long day. We betted alternately, and she shopped in between. That poor bookie would have liked to have killed both of us by the end of racing for the day. Every horse she named, won. We slept that night in the Balloch Hotel (in separate bedrooms) and dined off grouse pie like lords. I had two hundred pounds in my pockets, and God knew how much she had in hers. And Balloch is a good place to buy country clothes. She not only reappeared in anorak, new polo-neck sweater and very pukka climbing boots, but was able to change into a neat plaid skirt and stockings for dinner. Not bad for a girl who twenty-four hours ago had been stark naked. Now she was the utter lady; this waitress called her madam.

'I have enjoyed today,' she announced, as we parted for bed. 'I am going to enjoy it here, I think.'

'Where's *here*?' I said, suddenly and unwarrantedly hostile.

'Why, Scotland, of course,' she said.

She wanted to go on plundering the Balloch betting-shop the following day. We argued over it, at breakfast.

'We can't do it.'

'Why? It is not *illegal*.'

'Look, you'll make the poor sod bankrupt. There's a limit to what anybody can take, and he's only a little guy.'

'What is bankrupt?' There she went again; funny gaps in her knowledge. Like at dinner the previous night; she handled all the cutlery of a five-course meal far better than old peasant me, but when she dipped her pie into her little mound of salt, she went on getting it far too salty and pulling a face. As if she'd been taught all she knew of life in some school, and taught very well, but had been ill and missed some lessons altogether.

I tried again.

'We ought to go to a big town, where there are lots of big betting-shops that can stand the punishment . . .'

She thought, toying with the last of her bacon (she had a man's appetite to go with her size and strength), then nodded.

'What is the nearest big town?'

'Glasgow.'

'We will go to Glasgow.'

I wished I'd kept my mouth shut. I may be irrational, but I've always been terrified of that city. When I've passed through it, going climbing, I've always taken the direct bus from one outskirt to the other and never got off. I know people write to the papers about what a fine, warm city Glasgow is; about the noble Grecian architecture (black with soot) and the art gallery, and the Glasgow Orpheus Choir, but all I can think of is the Gorbals, and the gang-fights on the Easterhouse estate. I'd much rather have gone south to somewhere like Peterborough or Leicester, where I'm more at home. But there was no moving her. She had made up her mind. I found that out about her: if I wanted to change her mind, I had to give good reasons quick, before she'd announced her decision. Once she'd pronounced, her mind sort of locked.

You'll have noticed that by this time I had no further doubts about her power to pick winners. I was living in a crazy dream, where none of the usual rules worked; but by now I had got used to living in that dream. You can get used to anything, given forty-eight hours. So we took the bus to Glasgow and were soon ensconced in separate rooms in a very solid, respectable commercial hotel off Sauchiehall Street, run by a sharp body called Mrs Wemyss. Mrs Wemyss did not like our separate-rooms relationship, but Joan put on the queenly airs and totally charmed her. In fact, after that, every time I met Mrs Wemyss in the corridor, she'd look in the general direction of Joan's room and hiss in a loud stage whisper, 'She's a *real* leddy.'

Joan got straight down to the *Scotsman* with a pencil, and I worked out the strategy. We would visit the ten big betting-shops, and have a twenty-pound double at each. Joan picked two horses at ten-to-one odds. If they came up, we'd walk away with a cool twenty-five thousand pounds.

We walked; I did the betting. Women didn't go into Glasgow betting-shops much, except old biddies with carpet slippers, curlers and five pence each way on a Yankee. Joan would have stood out like a sore thumb, in her twin-set and plaid. And it seemed to go all right, though the last betting-shop had several characters hanging around who were more than just sleazy. They would have made a great white shark look like Florence Nightingale. And they gave me the eye. I hadn't realized then that telephones in betting-shops are not just for the benefit of people placing bets. Bookies talk to each other, about anything unusual . . .

Anyway, the two horses came up; I never expected they wouldn't. We went off to collect our winnings, and something, some twitching in my bones, made me insist on taking a taxi. It waited outside for us, while we collected. Even so, it was as well I took my rucksack; it's amazing just how bulky twenty-five thousand in notes is, and I wouldn't – couldn't – take cheques. Sometimes we had to keep the taxi waiting a long time, while they scratched together the notes. And I thought the cheerful way they paid up was a bit ominous.

The last shop was empty when I collected, which was a relief. It was less posh than the others, and the district it stood in was being allowed to run down into decay; half the houses were empty and the rest had gaping front doors, and groups of people sitting watching on their granite front steps. When I got outside, the taxi was gone; Joan was standing alone on the pavement, with the rucksack at her feet.

'What the hell . . .?'

'Two men came and took the taxi. They were in a terrible hurry to get to a friend lying dying in hospital—'

'Were they big guys,' I asked, 'with cropped hair and *boots*?'

She nodded. I began to feel *very* insecure. It was Glaswegian teatime; the smell of haggis cooking filled the greasy yellow air. Most of the porch-squatters had gone; no doubt standing by the family gas-stove with their skean dubhs at the ready. There was not a taxi in sight. Of course.

We started to walk. With every step the wads of notes on the Linen Bank of Scotland thumped and rustled seductively in the rucksack on my back. I felt the whole city must know about them. I was even flinching away when little girls passed, pushing toy prams. I wished I was home with my mum in Geordyland. I even wished I was sitting in my tent by Loch Lomond, eating wet bread and rotten plums.

'Do not worry,' said Joan. 'I will look after you.' I looked at her; she seemed in great form: glowing colour in her cheeks, an extra spring in her lovely athletic stride. Oh you poor innocent, I thought . . .

They stepped out of an alley between two warehouses, on the quietest part of the road home. I looked around hopefully, but there was no one within two hundred yards, and the only man in sight had his back turned. I considered shouting for help, looked at the three heavies and changed my mind. They gestured into the alleyway.

Joan stepped into the alleyway quite gaily, as if she was going on a school outing. All I could do was follow. *They* closed in behind. Joan, meanwhile, was not content to stop in the alley's mouth, where there was still a one per cent hope, such as a police car or a battalion of the Black Watch marching past. She walked right to the end of the alleyway and round the corner out of sight of the road. That even threw the yobs a bit. Too much of a good thing.

Joan turned and faced them. So did I. God, I never saw three faces I liked less. I could see they were busy planning to add the crime of rape to the crime of robbery with violence. And that would probably mean the crime of murder too. It seemed unfair; I was only twenty. They gestured to me to hand over the rucksack; they wouldn't want to risk getting the money splashed with blood.

Instead, Joan stepped forward, saying, 'What do you want?'

'Ye'll do for a start,' said the biggest one, reaching out a huge, grimy hand to grab her.

She made a movement then; very graceful, like the movement Sylvia used to make at tennis on the backhand, when the ball unexpectedly bounced too close to her. Next second, the biggest one was lying flat on his back, perfectly still. I mean, his chest was not going up and down. He did not seem to be breathing at all. It was absurd; such a little movement she had made; no noise, no blood. I couldn't believe any of it, standing there, paralysed, with the rucksack dangling from my hand.

The second man couldn't believe it either. He crouched, put out a hand gingerly to touch his friend.

'Get up, Tam, get up! Wha' the hell's the matter wi' ye? Get up, mon!' This mumbled monologue seemed to go on for ever, with nobody moving. Then he raised a scraped, bone-white face, incredulous, indignant.

'Ye've killed him, missus. Ye've killed him!'

She made the same graceful movement again, underarm this time. He collapsed gently across his friend.

The third man took to his heels. Joan was after him like a stoat after a rabbit. It had the same horrific fascination as a kill in a nature film; the same inevitability. At the last moment he turned and raised a helpless arm to protect his head. I felt a flash of pity for him then. She never touched his head . . . She came back, not even breathing heavily. She still had that glow in her cheeks; deeper, if anything. She took up the rucksack and walked away down another alley. All I could do was follow.

I caught up, and began to shout meaningless things at her. She gave me a look out of those steady blue eyes.

'Shut up. Do you want to spend the rest of your life in prison for men like *that*? Walk beside me normally. Control your breathing. Put your hand through mine. Aren't we supposed to be . . . lovers?'

I did as I was told. What else was there to do?

I tossed and turned in bed. The unbelievable scene in the alley played itself through and through my mind, like an ancient, silent newsreel that had never made sense even in the beginning.

The evening in the hotel had been awful. Sitting trying

to eat dinner. Trying to watch a succession of totally
meaningless TV programmes, and feeling I had gone insane.
The beady-eyed Mrs Wemyss had, of course, noticed. She
came across in her flowered overall, to ask if we'd enjoyed
our wee meal and added, 'Your young man's looking a bit
peaky . . .'

Joan gave her a charming full-face smile. 'My young man
and I have been having a frank talk. Just because we're going
to be engaged next week, and we're staying in a hotel, he's
been getting . . . certain ideas. I've explained to him I'm not
that kind of girl. He can wait till we're married. So now he's
sulking.'

Mrs Wemyss gave me an all-knowing look. 'That's the
way, hen,' she said to Joan. 'The men are all right . . . if they're
kept in their place. I was the same wi' Wemyss when we were
courting. I was brought up vairy pure; my family were Wee
Frees. Men'll always take advantage if they can. I say, what
they don't pay for, they don't appreciate.' The women smiled
at each other, conspiratorially. I damned them to hell, and
went to bed.

I heard my door open and close softly, and shot bolt
upright. The heavies' boss had tracked us down . . . the eagle-
eyed Glasgow CID . . .

It was Joan, standing in her white nightdress, with lace at
the throat and cuffs, looking like something out of a *Vogue*
Bridal Supplement. Enough to soften the hardest male heart.
She sat by me on the bed and took my hand. I thought
bitterly: if only your friend Mrs Wemyss could see you
now . . .

'Why d'you do it?' I spat at her.

'It was necessary.' She made it sound like a rough trip to
the dentist's.

'But . . . three? The other two would have run away.'

'And come back with their associates . . . Now, no one

knows who we are or where we are, or even if we did it. Did you not tell me that gangs fight and kill in Glasgow?'

'We should scarper . . .'

'That is what their friends and the police will be looking for; someone – as you say – scarpering. No one will look for us here. We will leave in two days' time.'

'They were *human beings* . . .'

'And what would these . . . human beings have done to me, if I hadn't stopped them?'

'Robbed you, raped you, killed you . . .'

'Well then. Now they can rob and rape and kill no more. Will not that make your world a better place?'

'*My* world . . .?'

She bit her lip, but recovered quickly. 'You know what I mean.'

'No, I don't know what you mean. What *do* you mean – *my* world?'

'The world you are so concerned about. You think too much.'

'What *are* you? CIA? KGB?'

She shook her head. 'I am . . . going to make you a millionaire, among other things.' Then, without warning, she stood up, pulled the nightdress over her head and got into the bed beside me. Her warmth was overwhelming, but my body still rebelled against what had happened, what she had done; and that she could do nothing about. Nevertheless, her warmth was a comfort and I must have fallen asleep at last. And by the time I was fully awake again, sometime in the dawn, it was all over. She was awake too, and lay looking at me, strangely, I thought. I got in a panic then.

'It's all *right*,' she said. With any other girl, that would have meant the safe time of the month. But there was something too . . . triumphant in this one's voice. She had done something she had planned to do. I remembered the Black Widow spider, who eats her mate afterwards. But she just got up and put on her nightdress, and ghosted away well before HMS *Wemyss*, that well-known Scottish battleship, could arise to say her prayers to St John Knox and get the breakfast.

There's no point in going into detail over what happened during the next three months. We bought a large motorized caravan, for cash and illegally, in a Glasgow used-car lot. I sussed out the caravans; Joan sussed out the dealers. I got us a useful Volkswagen Devon; Joan knew which dealer would take the hundred-pound bribe. Uncanny. We had to buy illegally because I'd only got a motorbike licence, and although Joan drove like a dream, the way she had arrived on my front doorstep precluded any chance of her having a licence tucked in her handbag.

We roved around England, only returning to one town so she could pass her driving test. She never liked being illegal more than was strictly necessary. And all the time we were placing bets and raking in cash, though she'd learnt caution now and we never took any bookie for more than he could bear. We built up massive accounts in bank after bank; then, by cunning transfers, she slowly gathered it all together in one account. You would have thought that some bright bank manager would have smelt a rat, but she sailed into each of their offices (in real pearls as well as the twin-set now) and charmed the pants off them with her royalty act. That was how I learnt the amazing fact that a girl of high breeding who underplays her legs and lace petticoat can addle the shrewdest male brain. Besides, who worries too much about a customer who is paying money *in*?

And pregnancy just ices the cake, when you're wearing a wedding ring – even if you haven't come by the ring legally. For yes, she was pregnant; in fact, by three months she was so hugely pregnant that she could hardly get behind the wheel of the van. I was appalled by what I'd done, raged and wept. She just smiled at me (she'd learnt to smile so well now, though she'd never smiled at first) and patted me on the head, as if I was a good little boy.

She began getting ready for the birth in a way that seemed precipitate even for the keenest first-time mum. By the end of the third month she had everything ready. But what really brought me out in a cold sweat was that she bought *three* of everything. I mean, three carrycots, three lots of nappies, three sets of feeding bottles. I asked her, rather sarkily, if she was expecting triplets, and she gave me that wide blue look and said, 'Of course. We always have three.'

'Who's *we*?' I shouted, a panic that was always with me suddenly surfacing, as it did at times.

'Our family, of course.'

'Who *are* your family? *Where* are they?'

She pulled a face. 'I had a row with them. You ought to be thankful. They'd get shot of you in a flash, for an ignorant yob.'

'Why don't you go and see a doctor?' I asked.

'It's not time yet,' she said, with another practised smile.

One wild October night, we parked the van on the hills above Porlock Weir. Autumn was upon us now, and the gusts of wind, carrying volleys of rain with them as they swept off Exmoor, set the van rocking, in spite of the shelter of a deep belt of trees. I was due to start back at college in three days; all summer long I'd fobbed off my parents with an assortment of postcards hinting vaguely at fruit-picking in Norfolk, or washing-up in Cornish hotels. Enough to dissuade them from reporting my disappearance to the police. But time was running out for me, and I was broody that night. She sensed it and tried to cheer me up by showing me our bank book.

'See? I've kept my word. You are a millionaire!' I stared at the number in the book. A one, and a row of noughts. I couldn't believe it, even though I'd often handled and counted greasy wads of five thousand quid in notes. I couldn't believe it, and at the same time it terrified me. A million quid, and three dead men . . . What *was* she? Most of the time I dumbly accepted her now; you can get used to anything after a while. But every so often I remembered what real life was like – work and sport and drinking with my mates, and then I would break out in a cold sweat and wonder what I was doing here.

'You could do with a drink,' she said, almost as if she'd read my thoughts. I suppose living together does that to people, after a bit.

'There's a nice pub down in Porlock Weir,' she said. 'I noticed it as we passed. Take an evening off. You've had too much of me, cooped up in this thing. Go on, relax!'

I fumbled in my pockets for money. She reached in her handbag and gave me five pound notes.

I had a good night; the ale was local, and the lads offered me a game of darts, hoping to win pints off me, which was their hard luck. Then we got talking bikes, and suddenly it was closing time and everyone vowing friendship like long-lost brothers. They left me where the road turns uphill.

It was pitch-dark; the gusts were getting stronger, though the rain had stopped. I thought of the van up there, rocking in the darkness, the windows curtained and gently lit with Calor-gas.

I didn't want to go back.

I didn't have to go back. I could just turn and walk the other way and get a hitch in the morning and be home by night with luck. It wouldn't be pleasant; I only had my anorak, and the rain might start again. But at least I would be home . . .

But my rucksack was up there, and one or two other things I valued. I was damned if I was going to let her have them. I staggered on; I was half-sloshed with the good ale, so it took a long and meandering time. But I made it at last. As I opened the van door, the wind nearly ripped it out of my hand and down the cliffs out to sea.

'Hurry up with that door,' she said, just like my mum talks to my dad. 'You'll have the place freezing. I'm doing you some coffee.'

I shut the door. Then I noticed the way she was standing. She was as slim as when I'd first seen her.

'What the hell . . .?' I said stupidly.

'Shhh,' she said. 'You'll wake them.' And on tiptoe, she went into the sleeping compartment at the back.

Three carrycots lay side by side on the floor; and in each of them, a child slept peacefully. They were big, for new-born babies. (I was godfather to my sister's, and this lot were bigger at birth than hers had been when it was christened at six weeks.) And they didn't look all screwed-up face and wizened either; they were beautiful, and their hair was the palest red-gold.

They didn't have a good effect on me; they did not bring out the fond father in me. In fact I turned on her.

'You scheming bitch – they're not mine!' I was filled with rage and hope at the same time. If they weren't mine, I had no responsibility to hold me here.

'They are yours,' she said softly. 'Look at their hair.' My hair is flaming red, and I'm proud of it.

'Who are you trying to kid? You must have been six months gone when you picked me up.'

'Did I look six months gone?' she asked softly. 'I'm the same again now.'

She took me again then, and the three golden babies wakened up noiselessly, without crying, and watched us.

22

Human kids can't focus their eyes until they're four months old.

When she was finished with me she got up and stretched like a cat, almost purring.

'I am . . . happy. I am not alone any more.' And she looked at the three babies, and they all opened their blue eyes again and looked back at her, as if they understood.

I pulled up the trousers she had undone (I was still wearing my damp anorak) and made a bolt for the door. She read my thought, but a second too late. Her hand grabbed my arm with fearful strength, but I slammed the van door on it and was away into the dark, sobbing and crying and panting as I ran. Behind me, I heard the van's engines start; the lights came on and caught me, as I dodged behind a hedge.

The rest was a nightmare. I ran and dropped, got my breath back and ran again. I don't know where I ran; sometimes I was in open fields, and sometimes crossing a road. Then I was among the sparse forest that sloped steeply towards the sea. And all the time, she was following me in the van; her headlights searched me out. I knew by this time that she could read my every thought, just as she could see the future and pick winners. But the terrain held her up: there are places a runner can go where a van can't. So I kept ahead, somehow. I was under no illusions about what she would do to me, if she caught me. Even if I was the father of all her brood. Black Widow spiders, here I come. I should have behaved myself, been a good little boy and gone on producing kids and money. Three kids every three months; and how long before the kids would start breeding themselves? These creatures – if they could be produced in three months – could be breeding at five years old. Their grandchildren would be breeding in ten years' time. With those brains, and looks, they could be running our world before I was an old man.

And somehow I knew they would always be female; males they could pick up here – any male would do. Though I supposed bright males would be preferred . . .

Bright? I suddenly realized with an awful conviction that the slope to the sea was getting steeper; turning into a cliff. I was on the cliff-edge itself, and, far below, the rocks were curdling the sea to foam. And at the same time I knew that I was standing in a clear space unprotected by trees or rocks; the van's lights pinned me like a butterfly to a board, as she closed in for the kill.

Something, I will never know what, made me give a last desperate leap to one side. I don't think I consciously timed it. Maybe God helped me, or some little wild cunning thing inside my mind that didn't want to die and knew better than me how to stay alive. The van caught me with its wing on the fat of my backside and flung me into some long grass. Paralysed with pain, I looked up as the van rushed past, curtained windows still lit and headlights blazing.

I don't think she miscalculated; not Joan: nor would she be too slow to put her foot on the brake. She would have had it worked out exactly. But maybe the ground was slippery with gravel there: maybe the old VW brakes had not been properly serviced, back in that crooked Glasgow car-dealer's yard.

The van almost halted, teetered. Then begun to plunge faster and faster. I think it turned over once, before it hit the sea; the headlights did a kind of cartwheel.

And then, though there was no sound over the wind and the waves, there was nothing left to be seen. Nothing at all. Joan, van, babies, bank book, cheques, million pounds, all gone. I was standing there in trousers and anorak, soaking wet. I remember feeling mad about my climbing boots and rucksack.

Then I turned and went back up a track to the road, and walked till dawn. I got a hitch at Minehead in a lorry going to

Bristol. I went home. My parents were pleased to see me. I watched the newspapers for nearly a year, but I never read anything. Maybe the sea is deep at the foot of that cliff, or the currents very strong.

I wonder if somewhere else, at this very moment, They're trying it on some sucker again.

If you see any naked blondes towards evening, mate, just bloody run.

BLACKHAM'S WIMPEY

Yes, I do fly in bombers. What's it like, bombing Germany? Do you really want to know? OK, brace yourself.

Two more pints, please, George.

Well, I expect you've been bombed by Jerry yourself. Plenty of bomb damage around. And there's you, sitting down in your shelter, behind your steel plate and three feet of earth, near wetting yourself and hoping the next bomb hasn't got your number on it. Well, being in a bomber's a bit like that, only the nasty bangs are coming up at you, instead of down.

But that's where any similarity stops. You see, a Wimpey – a Wellington bomber to you – isn't made of steel. It's made of cloth, stretched over a few aluminium tubes; a bit like a tent. If you try hard enough, and sometimes even when you're not trying, you can put your finger straight through the cloth and waggle it in the slipstream outside. So when a shell bursts near you, you can see the shell-splinters going right through your fuselage, like a horizontal shower of rain, and out the other side. I suppose I'm lucky, being the wireless operator; I've got two big radio sets to duck behind. Though by the time you've ducked, it's too late anyway.

And suppose you, down in your shelter, were sitting on about two tons of TNT just waiting for an excuse to blow up. And about a thousand gallons of petrol, in leaky tins that stink the place out, so you never dare light up a fag, however much you need one. And your air-raid shelter's in a bloody express lift that keeps going up and down without warning, so there's always a smell of spew about the place, even when your skipper's not taking violent evasive action. And you can't breathe properly without a dirty great mask over your face; and when you've got a head cold it's so bloody freezing you have to keep taking off your mask to knock an icicle off your nose.

No, it's not much like what you see on the movies.

And I think wireless ops have the worst job – because I am one. You can't see a thing that's going on, being sat right in the middle of the crate. There's bits of celluloid windows in the side, but they're brown with oil and smoke from the engines – they're never cleaned, not like the windscreen and gun-turrets. My oppo, the navigator, even he's got a little astrodome over his head. It's supposed to be for taking directions from the stars – doesn't that sound romantic? – but if he's ever reduced to navigating that way, we're really in trouble. He just uses it for being nosy, so he can add his two-pennyworth on the intercom.

Because it's the intercom that keeps us sane. You see, in a bomber, the only thing you can hear is the noise of the engines; it blots out even the racket of bursting flak. And you get so used to it, it gets to seem like silence – unless one of the engines starts to pack up, then you notice fast enough. But otherwise, when you're over target, you can see bomb-bursts and shell-bursts and flak-trails and even another crate buy it, and it's just like a silent movie, especially with your ears muffled up inside your helmet. But there's always the good old intercom, and all the lads yakking down it and even cracking mad jokes and laughing till the skipper shuts them up, like a teacher with a rowdy class. And it makes you feel not alone. And a good skipper keeps asking you every few minutes if you're OK, and that helps too.

My job's all listening, not looking. I have my eyes shut most of the time; might as well be blind. That's an idea, isn't it; blind wireless ops – save the fit men for the army? Anyway, as I said, my job's listening. I've got two radio sets: RT and WT. WT's for long-distance; Morse code only. It gives us directions from the top brass, like old Butcher Harris sitting on his arse at High Wycombe. And the only thing he'll tell you is to pack up and come home, 'cause the cloud's too thick to see the target, or maybe Fatty Goering's not at home that night 'cause he's sleeping at his aunty's. Now that's a little signal not to miss; if you do, you'll find yourself doing a solo raid on Berlin. Oh, I know that sounds great, like something out of the *Boy's Own Paper*, but actually it's not 'cause all over Europe there are little Jerry night-fighters sitting on their little nests of radar, just waiting for you to fly over slow as the morning milk cart. That's why we have these thousand-bomber raids: so Jerry'll have so many to think about, he'll run around in circles like a kid with presents on Christmas morning. Safety in numbers; if they're chopping some other poor sod, they're not chopping you. So I listen carefully for that little WT signal, which is not easy when the skipper's taking evasive action and the engines are doing their best to take thirty-six hours leave of absence from the wings, and our guns are going full blast and everyone's talking on the intercom at once. They're not supposed to, but try and stop them when the balloon's going up.

That's all about the WT, except you never use it. Jerry would get a fix on you in a flash; then you'd have company. Only time you use it is if you ditch in the sea coming home. Then you send out *Mayday* on five hundred kilocycles and hold the Morse-key down for thirty seconds to give them a fix on you. Trouble is, everybody's listening on five hundred kilocycles – air-sea rescue, German air-sea rescue, U-boats . . . take your pick. I've heard of lads freezing to death in the sea while two lots of silly buggers were fighting over them.

The RT – intercom in all your war movies – is a worry too.

You've got to keep the volume just right, see, so no one outside the crate hears a squeak. Turn the knob too far – easy enough done wearing icy gloves – and Himmler can hear you fart. I'm not shooting a line, honest!

So what keeps us going? Actually, we get a lot of laughs. Remember the time you and me were outside Beaky's study waiting to be caned, and we couldn't stop laughing? Well, it's like that all the time, almost. And we've got Dadda. Dadda's a great guy for laughs. Who's Dadda? the child asks. Dadda's our skipper – the big boss-man. Dadda's like God, only cleverer. Dadda has changed my life, the way God never did. I remember the first time we saw him.

We arrived at Lower Oadby one January dusk in '43. Flying Wimpey IIIs. Just the five of us, no Dadda then. The adjutant hadn't time to bother with us; there was an op on that night, so he just shoved us into a barrack-room with the crew of L-Love. L-Love were a bloody good crew – done twenty-two ops, but they weren't big-headed about it. They taught us a lot while they were getting kitted up. Things like always flying dead in the middle of the bomber stream because the Jerry fighters always nibbled at the edges. They weren't much older than us and made us laugh a lot, though we did wonder a bit why they looked so pale and sweaty; the barrack wasn't all that warm. And their rear-gunner was chewing gum so hard, his muscles kept standing out in knots all along his jaw. Anyway, they barged out saying don't do anything in Lower Oadby they wouldn't do. If you've seen Lower Oadby that's a big joke.

'They're OK,' said Matt, our only pilot, and we drifted across into their half of the barrack-room, inspecting their pin-ups and the photos of their girlfriends stuck on their lockers and touching their spare lucky silk stockings and rabbits' feet. Not being nosy; just looking and touching so that a bit of their luck would rub off on us. They'd shot down an Me 110, a twittish night-fighter that had flown slowly past them in the dark without even noticing they were there. Apparently it had blown up like the Fourth of July, and one of its prop-blades had lodged in L-Love's main spar without hurting anybody. Battered and rusting, it now hung over their skipper's bunk.

The hut was quiet and peaceful. We stoked up the stove till its stovepipe glowed cherry-red halfway to the ceiling, and we all snored off like babes.

The barrack-room door banged open with a gust of snow at four in the morning. Somebody shoved on all the lights.

'Good shopping trip?' shouted Billy the Kid, our rear-gunner, always first with a wisecrack. We all sat up.

It wasn't them. It was three stupid-looking RAF police with snow on their greatcoats. Carrying big canvas sacks in each hand. They didn't say a word to us, just started grabbing all L-Love's kit and golf clubs and spare rabbits' feet and stuffing them into the sacks. Ripping down the pin-ups off the lockers.

'Hey!' shouted Matt. 'What the hell you doing?'

One of the police turned to him, his face blank as a Gestapo thug's just before he pulls the trigger. 'They got the chop,' he said. 'Tried to land at Tuddenham and overshot the runway.' He turned away and began throwing stuff into his bags with renewed vigour. None of them looked at us again. We sat up in bed in our striped pyjamas, hating them. Until they tried to take the prop-blade off the wall. Then Matt was out of bed in a flash.

'Leave that alone. That's ours.'

The policeman reached for the blade.

'It's ours, I tell you!' screeched Matt. 'They *gave* it to us.'

'Yeah,' we all yelled. 'They *gave* it to us.'

The policeman shrugged. He knew we were lying. But

Matt's a big lad and he was mad as hell. They finished stuffing stuff into bags and left, jamming off the lights.

'Bastards,' said Matt, getting back into bed.

'They're only doing their job,' said Kit, the navigator. 'I don't expect they like doing it, over and over again.'

'Some guys enjoy being undertakers . . .'

Nobody said anything for some time. Then, in the dark, Kit said, 'They were a good bunch. I'm glad they all went together.' Which was a pretty bloody stupid thing to say, but what isn't bloody stupid on that kind of occasion?

Billy the Kid went out to the bogs and was very sick. We listened. In a way he was being sick for all of us; saved us getting out of bed.

We kept the prop-blade a week, then threw it away. It sort of filled the whole hut, like the evil eye of the little yellow god. We never tried interfering with those policemen again, except once.

Next morning, they ran us down to the dispersals to see our new crate, C-Charlie. She really was brand-new, which was funny. They normally give green crews the clapped-out old crates. Why waste a good bomber on a mob who are five times more likely to get shot down than anybody else?

It was bloody freezing, even wearing two sets of long johns and a greatcoat. We mooched around her, kicking things and grumbling; feeling totally unreal and farting and belching all over the crate and giggling every time. Does that shock you? It was partly, I suppose, to show how we felt about everything, and partly to try and get something hard and solid out of our guts which would never go away again. You probably know, that's the way fear feels. And Billy the Kid kept bleating plaintively about who the other pilot would be.

'Me,' said Matt. 'There is no other pilot. They're trying to *save* pilots.'

'If they blew this bloody crate up now, they could save a navigator as well. And a wireless op and two air-gunners and a lot of petrol.' Kit was the real joker, even then. Life and soul of the party. Only, his big blue eyes were stary that morning, the whites showing all round like they seldom have since.

We dropped back on to the tarmac.

'I always wanted to be a landgirl,' said Matt. Since he was six foot two and the only one of us who had to shave every day, it was *quite* funny.

We stood and talked and froze. We found out that a year ago, we'd all been in the sixth form. We found out that Matt had been the top pilot of his course, and Kit top navigator. Mad Paul, the front-gunner, and Billy the Kid were top stuff, too; reaction times like greased lightning. (They played a stupid game involving slapping each other's hands; anyone else who joined in always lost, and it really hurt.) Only I was mediocre. I had passed-out halfway down the wireless ops' list.

Still we stood. Were we all there was? Was Matt's horrible idea coming true? Did we have to take this thing to Germany on our own?

Just then a thirty-hundredweight drove up. A pair of long, thin legs emerged from the cab, stooped shoulders and a cap pushed back to display a wrinkled forehead and balding nut. He didn't look at us; he walked across to C-Charlie with the precarious dignity of a heron hunting frogs. We gaped at the apparition. His uniform, which carried wings and a flight-lieutenant's rings, was thin and grey as paper.

'Look at that uniform,' said Matt, not bothering to lower his voice. 'He's got some time in.'

'Probably in the pay office,' said Kit.

'You can make blues look like that over a weekend,' said Billy. 'Bit of bleach in the water, and a razor-blade to scrape the fluff off . . .'

The apparition kicked the starboard tyre violently, stalked on and began doing a Tarzan-act on the starboard flaps. The Wimpey is a pretty whippy, flexible sort of plane. Some pilots compare flying one to lying in a hammock, others to making love to a woman. The steering-column keeps nudging your chest, the engines nod up and down in a regular rhythm and the wing tips actually flap in flight. This guy had the whole plane rocking in motion, the way he was thumping hell out of her.

'Shall I go and tell him it's government property?' asked Matt. We all got those stupid giggles again. The apparition ignored us, until he had given the tail-wheel a final kick. Then he walked over to us.

He knew we'd been taking the mickey. He found us amusing.

'Let's get you into your bunny-suits,' he said, 'and see if this thing flies.' We bundled into the back of his thirty-hundredweight, all except Matt, who he kept with him in the front. All I will say about the way he drove is that I was sick halfway back to the billet. Of course, I was sitting over the exhaust.

'If he flies like he drives,' said Kit, 'we won't make the coast.'

'The German coast?' I gasped, pulling my head back in over the tailboard.

'The English coast,' said Kit.

New flying-kit has a life of its own. It makes you feel like a giant panda, trussed up for its journey to the zoo. It trails things that wrap around any knob or lever available; it makes you a yard wide so you knock things off shelves that you think are miles away. Passing anybody else in the confines of a Wimpey is like dancing with a stuffed bear. You feel sweaty and cut off from everything.

Dadda's gear wasn't like that. He had battered all the life out of it; it fitted him like a second skin. In places it was creased and wrinkled like rhinoceros hide; in other places it was worn smooth and shiny. There were great dirty patches near the most-used pockets. He looked more like a decrepit heron than ever.

We took off smoothly and easily. Piece of cake, I thought. Then he told me I had too much volume on the intercom, though I don't know how the hell he knew. Then he told Kit he talked too much. I was still laughing silently about that when the WT set hurled itself violently into my side; lots of painful knobs too. Next second, I was dangling, helpless, in the middle of the fuselage on the end of my safety-harness. Next second, I got the distinct impression I was hanging upside down. Certainly three pencils and a map shot up in front of my face.

I was sick again, and now there was no tailboard to lean out over. Further forward, the Elsan toilet broke loose with a terrific clatter and came sailing past my head. Thank God it was empty. First I thought my last moment had come, then I hoped it had. When I got myself together a bit, Dadda told me to turn the intercom up. I was just reaching for the knob when the world turned upside down again. I heard Kit say, in a dreamy voice,

'He *can't* fly upside-down at zero feet.' Kit had somehow strapped and braced himself so he could look out of the astrodome. 'I can see ducks sitting in mud over my head.' His face was lit up like a child's at a funfair. After that, all I did was to keep my eyes shut, play with the intercom knob, and try to keep my guts inside me. And listen to Kit's running commentary.

'I think we're strafing Spalding . . .

'Two cars have just crashed . . .

'He's knocked three bricks off a factory chimney . . .

'We're flying down a canal – below the level of the banks . . .'

Mind you, I wouldn't swear to the truth of any of it. Kit always shot a line, given the least chance. But it *felt* like it. And there was a lump of bracken caught in our closed bomb-doors afterwards; that even Kit couldn't have faked.

We finally reached the ground and crawled out. Dadda began belting hell out of the crate again, this time in the company of the ground-crew sergeant, and not sounding too pleased.

'He can fly,' said Matt judiciously. 'But only Spitfires.'

'Can't you tell him this one's got two engines?' added Billy plaintively.

'He's mad,' said Mad Paul. That, from Mad Paul, was approval.

'I don't know what he does to the enemy,' said Kit, 'but by God he frightens me.' He lit a Woodbine and did his impersonation of an aircrew-recruiting poster, a foot nonchalantly on the Wimpey's undercart as if he'd shot it himself.

I was sick again, over the undercart, and his foot. It was the only comment I could make. All those silly buggers' eyes were shining, as if it was Christmas. Already they were calling the flight the Battle of Spalding.

I set my mind to finding out more about this nut of a pilot. I wanted to know who was killing me.

His name was Townsend. He was an Irishman, a Dubliner. Spoke that lovely clear English that only a certain type of Irishman speaks. When he said 'the Castle' he meant Dublin Castle. He was a Catholic; drove (like the devil) every Sunday morning to an ugly little yellow-brick Catholic church in Wisbech. It was the only thing he didn't joke about. They said he'd spent two years at Maynooth, intending to be a priest and then a monk. But he'd left, saying it made the years too long. That's why they started calling him Father Townsend, which got shortened to Dadda. At least, that was the story. Maybe they only called him Dadda because he was so much older than the rest of us. Thirty-five if he was a day.

After Maynooth, he seemed to have drifted. He taught English in some kind of left-wing free-school in Germany, till the Nazis closed it down. He'd seen Hitler before Hitler became famous; talked about him with neighbourly Irish spite as a busy, worried little man in a crumpled, belted raincoat. Somehow, that cut Hitler down to size for us. Later, Kit started the 'Paddy O'Hitler' craze that was unique to C-Charlie, though other crews tried copying us. Night-fighters became Paddy O'Hitler's chickens. Bremen Docks, on fire, became Paddy O'Hitler's rickyard.

'Rickyard's well alight tonight, Dadda!'

'Maybe Paddy won't be able to pay this quarter's rent.'

'Maybe the great landlord in the sky will evict him.'

'Chicken dead astern, Dadda.'

'Wring its bloody neck,' said Dadda dreamily, as he fell down the sky in his famous corkscrew, and the Elsan broke loose again. Half-full this time, and everybody laughing like drains. Over a silly childish game. But op by op the game kept us laughing; kept us alive. And maybe Billy did wring a couple of chickens' necks.

After he'd lost his German job, Dadda seemed to have drifted on round the English Catholic schools, teaching languages. Never staying long. Until the war came, and he learnt to fly. This was his third tour of ops. You only had to fly one. Most crews didn't last half a tour before they got the chop. People said Dadda'd survived because he didn't care if he lived or died; that was the way things went. People said that when the war was over, there'd still be one Wimpey flying over Europe in the dark, with Dadda at the controls, wondering where the war had gone to. They said he was mad as a hatter; flew like a lunatic.

They didn't know him. Actually, he didn't miss a trick. Every day we polished the perspex of our own turrets and windscreens, and he inspected them. 'A fingerprint's bigger than a night-fighter, *acushla*. We don't want chickens hiding behind fingerprints.'

On a raid, he always flew dead in the middle of the bomber stream. But at his own chosen height, which never appeared in Air Ministry Regulations. Three thousand eight hundred feet. That's a very healthy height. The light flak's lost its sting, and the heavy flak – the 88s and 102s – is unhappy and slow. And any night-fighter has got the ground and church steeples on hills to worry about, as well as you. Especially if it tries to attack from underneath, which is a favourite stinking little trick.

Besides, three thousand eight hundred feet gave Mad Paul the chance to have a crack with his front guns at the light-flak gunners and the searchlight-crews. I dare say it didn't do Jerry much harm, but it did Paul a lot of good. Gave him something to do; left him no time to think. Time to think you do not need; people die of it. Dadda kept everybody busy. He let Matt really fly the crate, once he knew how. Didn't just leave him sitting and sweating like a stuffed duck, which happens to some second-pilots. Kit was kept busiest of all: new readings, new courses, hot coffee all round; it suited him. Dadda even found something for me.

'I've got you a new box of tricks, *acushla*. A little beauty called Tinsel.' Tinsel was a third radio, which I could use to search out the Jerry fighter-control network. There was a crawling fascination in hearing the voices from Tomtit and Bullfinch, earnest German voices trying so hard to shoot us down. Then, at the crucial moment, I could black out their transmission by sending them the sound of our starboard engine, neatly recorded by a microphone in the engine-nacelle. God, it made those Jerries hop and swear. I tell you, and I'm not shooting a line, I've got the best collection of German obscenities in the RAF.

'How did you know I spoke German, Dadda?'

'Read it up in your records, *acushla*, before you were a twinkle in Groupie's eye . . .'

We had a private joke, too – Dadda and I. Any time a night-fighter got on our tail, I was to shout, 'You stupid Dummkopf, Otto, can't you see I'm a Heinkel in disguise?'

I think it was when he first suggested this, and I laughed till I was nearly sick, that Dadda became a kind of God, even to me.

The business about Blackham's Wimpey started the night we raided Krefeld; at ops tea. Ops tea is the special meal they give you before you go over Germany. Best meals we ever got. Usually a heap of bacon and fried bread and two whole precious fried eggs. Trouble is, even if you're in a good mood, you keep thinking: the condemned man ate a hearty meal; and if you're feeling rotten you feel you're a pig being fattened up for slaughter. The fried bread turns to sawdust in your mouth, the fried eggs turn to glue, and the edges of the crispy bacon start burrowing into the lining of your stomach. But you get your ops tea down somehow. It may be the last thing you touch before you do your flaming-torch act; except for a face-wash of lukewarm coffee, halfway across the North Sea.

Crews sit together at ops tea, always. Even if they hate each other the rest of the time. Everybody's life depends on everybody; there's no room for hate. Love, or you're a dead duck. Instant Christianity. Did you know, someone actually wrote a book for aircrews called *God Is My Co-pilot*? You used to find copies in the bogs, with half the pages gone. Anyway, crews sit together. And they're either very noisy or very quiet. If they're quiet, people reckon they're on the chop list. We do a lot of wondering who's on the chop list. Certain barrack-huts lose crew after crew. Falling in love is fatal. There was one gorgeous WAAF in the parachute store; none of us would even speak to her. Anybody who looked twice at her got the chop.

Anyway, this night we were sat next to Blackham's lot. We didn't like Blackham's lot, though, looking back, I can see that the only thing really wrong with them was Blackham. Colin Blackham, their skipper. Blackham the bastard. In civvy-street, he was a Yorkshire hill farmer, a real Yorkshire tyke. Pig-ignorant and hard with it, with a hill farmer's attitude to life and death. Would send his granny to the knacker's yard, if the price was right. Bradford Grammar had dragged him through school certificate, and he never forgave them for it. Well over thirty, nearly as old as Dadda, he was still only a flight-sergeant, and he made a loud-mouthed virtue of it. Always started arguments with 'Well, I'm only a flight-sergeant, but . . .' And every time you saw him he was arguing. Horrible sober and worse drunk. A long, bony jaw and a big nose and beady dark eyes, and a hill farmer's broken veins in his cheeks, and black hair that escaped the Brylcreem after five minutes and stood out all over his head in greasy spikes. He always wore a filthy white polo-neck sweater that not only showed under his BD top but came down nearly to his knees. The best thing about him was, he was pretty small. A little bullock who would always settle a logical argument with his fists, if he was losing. Even after what happened to him, I still hate him.

As I said before, Blackham's lot were next to us and making even more noise than usual. They all mimicked Blackham, like we all mimicked Dadda. They were discussing that stupid Air Ministry instruction about machine-gunning farm animals on the way back from raids. To undermine Adolf's war effort. Of course, most crews ignored the instruction. We all had a shrewd idea what we were doing to women and children in the German cities, but we didn't have to look at it, and we didn't talk about it either. But being told to kill horses and cows in broad daylight . . . Anyway, if it was light enough and you were low enough to shoot at farm animals, you'd better save your ammo for the fighters.

Dadda hated the idea, and, being Dadda, mocked it. He worked out it cost us more for the ammo than it cost Adolf for the cow, and Adolf got to eat the cow anyway. But Blackham's lot loved the idea; went in for it (if you could believe them) in a big way. Last time out, they said, they shot at a Belgian girl herding cows and not only killed the cows but her dog as well; *and* made her dive into a ditch so fast, they saw the colour of her knickers. By now Blackham's face was red and sweating. His noise was stirring up the whole mess-hall. Some tables were giving him dirty looks, others were starting to tap out Morse code with their knives and forks, or gouging bloody great chunks out of the table-tops. It was unbearable.

So I said, 'Aah, shut your face, Blackham.' Loud enough for everyone to hear. Next second I wished to hell I hadn't.

There was a horrible silence. Blackham turned to me slowly.

'Did you say something to me, son?'

I couldn't open my mouth.

'No,' said Dadda, 'I did. I requested you to shut your face, Flight-sergeant Blackham.'

Blackham looked from one to other of us, baffled. He wasn't stupid; he knew who'd said it. But he was frightened of a trap.

'Yes,' said Kit. 'I distinctly heard our honourable skipper request you nicely to shut your face, *Sergeant* Blackham. Is that not so, gentlemen?' He turned to us.

'Yeah,' said Billy.

'Beyond any reasonable doubt,' said Matt.

'Indubitably,' said Mad Paul.

Blackham got to his feet with a heave that sent his mob scattering. Dadda sat still, laughing at him. One poke at Dadda, and the squadron would have lost Blackham for good. The noise of drumming fists and knives and forks from the other tables was thunderous.

'Flight-lieutenant Townsend. A word with you!' And there was Groupie, smiling his smile of pure ice. Groupie was a hero; bagged four Jerries, they said, in World War One. Didn't use his single synchronized Vickers gun; *froze* them out of the sky with his famous smile. Anyway, he came across and put his arm round Dadda's shoulders and held a perfectly fatuous conversation about the stirrup pump and fire buckets in 'B' flight office. Somebody down the mess-hall gave a loud snore; but when Groupie looked up, the wise lad was finishing off his eggs.

Krefeld was no worse than usual. The PFs – Pathfinders – seemed to have stayed sober for once and had dropped a new kind of marker: a bright red ring of fires that even the incompetent were able to get their bombs into. There was a smell of burning silk and disturbed chemicals in our share of the atmosphere over the target. Better than the Sunday-lunch smell you get from burning city centres. Matt saw a Lanc buy it overhead; a shell from a 102 blew its wing off. We were glad it was a Lanc, and not anybody we knew. Those toffee-nosed bastards actually cheer when they hear we're on a raid with them. We're sent in first, you see, and we fly slower and lower, so we're easier targets. I mean, a Lanc can carry five times our bomb load, so why do they send us at all, except as bait for the flak and fighters?

On the way home we met clouds, thank God. It had been a clear sky all the way to Krefeld, and a three-quarters moon, and we'd felt as if we were doing a striptease in Adolf's front garden.

Now skippers react differently to clouds. Some get inside and stay inside, even when the clouds are cu-nimbus. The buffeting inside cu-nim can bash a damaged plane to bits, and all that static electricity doesn't exactly mix with a crate full of petrol fumes . . . And you might meet somebody you know inside. A Wimpey's wing-tip can kill you just as dead as a cannon shell. And the fighters can still track you on their radar and jump you when you come out blind.

Other skippers fly up the cloud canyons, as visible as a black fly on a tablecloth. OK, black night-fighters are easily spotted, too, but who's biggest and most visible, and who's looking for who?

Dadda sort of flirted with the clouds; up and down the slopes, around the pinnacles, in and out like a flipping skier. It was fascinating and almost *cleansing*, after the flames and smell at the target. A bit like having a cold shower after a rugger match. Not a soul in sight; might as well be flying over the North Pole.

But believe me, Dadda wasn't flirting with the clouds to refresh his soul. Unless we were getting a star-fix, Dadda never flew in a straight line for ten seconds at a time. They said he'd once scrounged a ride with RAF Beaufighters and knew just what makes a night-fighter careworn; besides, he said his constant stunting kept the crew awake. It's fatally easy to doze off, once you've left the target, and many a poor rear-gunner has departed this life lost in a frozen dream of hot crumpet. Other idiots play dance-music on their WT.

'Dadda, you're getting too far south – out of stream. Steer 310.'

Dadda banked to starboard, and there was a twitchy silence

on the intercom, apart from Billy muttering, 'Nothing . . . nothing . . . nothing,' to himself as he swung the rear-turret from side to side.

'We bring nothing into this world,' said Kit, making eyes at me over his oxygen mask. 'And it is certain we shall take nothing out.' Honestly, that kid would roller skate round the jaws of hell, laughing.

'Shut up,' said Dadda.

'Wimpey at three o'clock,' said Billy. 'Beneath you.' It was lucky he said Wimpey, and not crate or kite, because before he could have corrected his mistake Dadda would have corkscrewed down a thousand feet, and we'd have lost the Elsan again. I stuck my head up into the astrodome alongside Kit's. Dadda was banking the crate to get a good look, so we got a good look too.

'S-Sugar,' said Matt.

'Blackham,' said Mad Paul. 'Seven hundred bombers out tonight and we have to get Blackham.'

'Anyone watching the rest of the sky?' asked Dadda sharply.

There *was* something compelling, eye-catching, about that black Wimpey stooging straight up the cloud canyon, its big squadron letters glinting in the moonlight, its blue moon-shadow skating across the cumulus below.

'Looks like a ghost ship . . . like the *Mary Celeste*,' I said out loud.

'What d'you expect them to be doing – holding a candle-light dance?' said my good and honoured oppo.

On and on we flew three hundred yards apart. It was protection of a sort. If a night-fighter found us, he couldn't attack both at once. Raised the odds to fifty-fifty. I saw the other Wimpey's rear-turret swing towards us once or twice, winking in the moonlight. Whether he was just keeping a good watch, or putting up the two fingers of scorn at us . . .

Dadda was still dodging in and out of the clouds. We kept losing and finding Blackham. I had a terrible temptation to turn up the intercom and say something to them.

People have died for less.

But it was company in a way, in all that empty sky. If I'd been pilot, I'd have wanted to huddle close.

People have died for less.

'This astrodome makes your ears bloody cold,' said Kit, and went back to his navigator's table, leaving me to it. We could fly on and on for ever, under the moon, I thought. Across the Atlantic and breakfast in America. If the fuel held out . . . which it wouldn't.

It was a moment before I saw it; and another moment when I didn't believe my eyes; then a moment when the blood pounded into my head and I sweated all over. Blackham's Wimpey had *two* blue shadows now; flitting beneath it on the cloud floor. How could a Wimpey have two shadows, when there weren't two moons?

Then one of the shadows, the smaller one, changed its angle and began to climb up beneath Blackham. Rising like a ghostly shark out of the cloud depths. Then the cockpit of the shadow glinted, and I saw it for what it was: a Junkers 88. The one the Germans call 'Owl'; mottled blue-grey skin, the bristling nose-whiskers of the Lichtenstein radar, the twin black muzzles of the upward-pointing *Schräge Musik* cannons behind the cockpit. Nearer and nearer it climbed, towards the soft underbelly of the Wimpey. I croaked. I whimpered.

I banged the intercom wide open and yelled, 'Blackham – corkscrew port – fighter below you!'

Blackham didn't need telling twice. His bomber turned into a great black cross as he banked before diving. Even then, I thought he was too late. A sudden thread of golden fire tied Junkers and Wimpey together like an umbilical cord; from the tail of the Wimpey to the centre-section of the Junkers.

But when the flames came, they blossomed from the Junkers. Blackham's twist to port must have brought the Junkers momentarily into the field of fire of his rear-turret. The turret-guns must have been pointing in the right direction by sheer chance, and the gunner touched his buttons as a nervous reflex to something so close. Pure fluke. But enough. Next second, Blackham was cartwheeling down the sky in his defensive corkscrew like an insane crow. And the Junkers was describing a beautiful parabola of flame upwards.

I still don't understand what happened next. I don't think my opening up of our intercom alone could have caused it. I can only think it was some kind of electronic hiccup. But suddenly our intercom was full of alien voices.

'I got the bastard! I *got* him!' That was Geranium, Blackham's rear-gunner.

'You sure?' Blackham's voice, tense and very Yorkshire-tyke.

'Sure I'm sure. See him burn!'

Wild cheers from Blackham's lot.

Then a German voice. 'Bullfinch Three to Bullfinch. Abandoning aircraft. Port wing on fire. Get the hatch open, Meissner! Meissner, get the hatch open. Ritter, help him!'

We listened, appalled, as the Junkers continued to burn and continued to fly wildly across half the sky, somehow keeping pace with us, arching its beautiful parabolas of fire.

'Meissner, Ritter! What's holding you up? Are you dead?'

The Junkers, by some trick of fate, was now flying almost level with us, almost parallel. So we saw the flames from the wing creep up the fuselage, and the cockpit-canopy shrivel away under its licking. And the orange-lit face of the pilot staring at us, out of the flames, aghast.

Then the Junkers was gone, falling, falling.

'Watch the rest of the sky,' said Dadda automatically. But none of us could tear our eyes away from the Junkers below.

Because that was when the flames must have reached him.

He screamed. It should have been his death-scream. But then the flames must have let go of him again, like a cat lets go a half-dead mouse. We could hear him whimpering as the Junkers, incredibly – flying like a singed moth, a half-swatted fly – climbed slowly back to our level.

This time, he noticed us. Maybe he blamed us for all his troubles. He made a frenzied attempt to ram us, screaming, '*Heil Hitler! Sieg Heil, Sieg Heil, Sieg Heil.*' At least I think it was that, among the bubblings from his burnt nose and mouth and lungs. He sounded more like a half-slaughtered animal than a man; except nobody would ever do that kind of thing to an animal.

Dadda, half-paralysed for once by the approach of that terrible apparition, took evasive action just in time. The Junkers' slipstream battered us down the sky; we felt his heat and smoke billowing in through every nook and cranny; and that awful smell, just a hint, or maybe I only imagined it. Over the intercom, Blackham's lot were still laughing; laughing at him, laughing at us.

'Burn, you bastard, burn!'

Unbelievably, the Junkers began to overtake us again. Christ, he might blow up at any moment, wrapping us in a shroud of red-hot gas that would be his fuel and his glycol and his ammo and his flesh. I pulled my chute to me and began clipping it on. We were always more afraid of fire than anything else, in those old cloth bombers. Especially of our own chutes catching fire, so that when we baled out we flared up like comets. He still kept after us. He was rambling in his mind, now. Calling on his radar-controller one minute, his mother the next.

'*Mutti, Mutti.*' Telling his mother he didn't have a left hand any more, that his charred fingers had broken off on the control-column. Three times, in between the flames catching him, he gave his name, rank and number, clear as clear.

'73794 Leutnant Gehlen, Dieter Ernst.'

Once he cried, 'My eyes, my eyes!'

And all the time, in the background, Blackham's lot were laughing. (I heard afterwards that Dadda told me three times to turn down the intercom, and I never even heard him.)

He blew up at last, well below us and about a mile behind. Long trails of pink and white burning stuff shot in every direction, as if someone had set off a bundle of Guy Fawkes rockets. Then the sky was black, till the moon returned to our senses.

'Get that intercom turned down, Gary. I'm tired of telling half Germany where I am.'

'Yes, Dadda.' We had been flying three minutes on a straight course, sending out radio-signals clear as lighthouse beams. We were *dead*. Dadda went into the steepest dive I have even been in. We fell like a stone. I thought we would never pull out; I thought we were mortally hit, though I hadn't heard a sound.

We came home at zero feet, and, until we cleared the Belgian coast, on petrol-guzzling full boost. Zero feet with Dadda meant just that; I saw at least three church steeples flick by overhead. It felt better that way. When you're high up, you feel big as a haystack and slow as a cow. At zero feet, you feel powerful, like a crazy, souped-up racing car. We were almost part of the ground. Smells of the earth wafted through the fuselage for a second, and were gone. You always get your share of the local atmosphere in a Wimpey. And the smells were a sort of sad comfort; the sharp tang as Dadda clipped the tips of a pine forest, then the rich smell of a pig farm. Once, enough to make you cry, the safe, warm smell from an early-working Belgian bakery. We saw no more fighters; none saw us. Perhaps they were all chasing Blackham. Maybe there was still some justice in the world, ha-ha. Two miles beyond the coast, a flak-ship opened up on us with tracer; red and green balls, very pretty, very slow-curving, then accelerating alarmingly. Here's ours, I thought. Here we go to join Gehlen at the gates of hell. But they'd misjudged our range or speed. The tracers passed miles behind us.

When we landed at Lower Oadby, S-Sugar was already standing in her dispersal-pen. And the debriefing hut was swamped with the noise of Blackham's lot. You always get a horrible tot of RAF rum at debriefing; it smelt and sounded as if Blackham's lot had joined the rum queue several times each. They had simply flown home, without taking any evasive action. Four times they'd been attacked by fighters, but, according to Blackham, they'd been 'Waiting for the little bastards, just waiting for them.' They were claiming two more kills, and were giving the little WAAF who was debriefing them a hell of a time.

'Here's a lovely lad'll confirm one,' said Blackham, grabbing both my cheeks between his fingers and thumbs. 'He gave it to me, didn't you, me lovely lad? Ah was going to *nail* thee, but now us is quits. When tha tell the young lady Ah roasted one o' them bastards over a slow fire.' I was sick all down his flying-jacket; and I was never less sorry about anything in my life. I blundered out of the debriefing hut; the light and heat and the noise were like some Viking feast . . . I'd heard that all Yorkshire tykes were Vikings in the beginning.

Dawn was just starting to break; the runways, the parked Wimpeys were like pencil-scrawls on a lavatory wall; meaningless garbage. How ungrateful can you get? I thought. Dadda's brought us home by a miracle, and I'm not even glad. Because tomorrow night, or the next, or the next, we shall be going back to do it all over again. Anyway, I wasn't home on the airfield; I was still sitting in that burning cockpit with Gehlen. He had sounded about our age . . . I was back with Gehlen, over and over and over again. Life had stopped with Gehlen, like a faulty gramophone record that keeps the needle jumping back to the same place and repeating the same tune. Bugger the Germans and the British. There were just those who flew three miles high on a load of petrol and explosives, and those who didn't. That was the real difference: those that flew and those that sent them.

I realized the lads had gathered round me, silently, in their soft flying-boots. We looked at each other, then looked away. Gehlen was in Matt's eyes, in Kit's, in Billy's eyes that looked like burnt holes in a white sheet. We'd had it. We were on the chop list and we knew it, just as we'd been before Dadda arrived.

'Let's go and hunt up some ham-and-eggs,' said Dadda. It wasn't an invitation; it was an order. We piled listlessly into the thirty-hundredweight, and he drove off, slowly.

It was very quiet crossing the Fens; the trees were the faintest possible silhouettes, the sky was flushing a pale pink, nothing like Krefeld, and the birds were just starting to sing. We passed an old farmhand, who wobbled on his bike in our slipstream, but waved just the same. And, slowly, the miracle happened, as it had happened before. The birdsong began to seep into our minds, then the silhouettes of the trees; like water seeping into a leaky old boat. We were back in the here and now, in a beautiful little nowhere; content to be there, and not to think at all. Gehlen began to fade. Oh, he still came, played over and over again, but the birdsong and the trees diluted him. Slowly, gradually, he got weaker and weaker. Dadda didn't hurry; he wasn't doing twenty miles an hour: the thirty-hundredweight bumped its springs over the uneven Fenland roads as gently as a cradle. Matt's cocked-up leg relaxed and slid slowly across the metal bed of the lorry. Paul sighed and wriggled his shoulders back and forward. Kit let his head bounce on his hand where it lay on the tailgate, obviously enjoying the feeling.

Dadda had found the ham-and-eggs farm after a hairy forced landing in a Whitley in 1941. He had left his rear-gunner in charge of the wreck, and just walked into the farmhouse. I suppose the famous Dadda smile did the rest, though people would do anything for somebody in flying gear, in those days just after the Battle of Britain. You could sit and watch the farmer's wife cutting slices of ham off the joint, which hung up on a beam when it wasn't in use. If you had the energy, you could go out to the hen cree with the farmer's kids, and push the hens off the nesting-boxes and take your own personal eggs straight from the straw, still warm. There was never ham-and-eggs like Dadda's ham-and-eggs. The eggs didn't turn to glue in your throat and the edges of the ham left the lining of your stomach alone. And after breakfast you could mooch round the farmyard, watching the milk squirt into the galvanized bucket as the farmer milked each cow by hand. Kick the horse manure and smell the pong coming off it. Or listen to the farmer's wife getting aerated about the Ministry of Ag. and Fish. inspectors. Those farmers were so caught up in their little world, they never thought to ask about ours. Sometimes they asked us to lend a hand, cleaning out a byre. If we had nothing better to do. Because we had the day off, hadn't we? The *whole* day off? they asked enviously.

God bless their ignorance; it washed us clean.

Before we left, I took a couple of leaves from a plant that grew in the garden. When you rubbed them between your finger and thumb, they gave off a minty, lemony smell. The farmer's wife said a couple of leaves under your pillow helped you sleep. I went back to the billet with mine, and slept like a baby.

Next raid, our flight was sent on a diversionary attack, on the docks at Lorient. For once, Lorient was a soft job, practically a milk-run. Dadda took us in at zero feet all the way. Lucky it was a calm night; we still came back with a length of seaweed stuck on the cockpit-canopy. But he got past the flak-ships without a murmur, and under the German radar, and because we hadn't got to waste time gaining height we arrived ahead of the bomber stream. We had Lorient to ourselves, dumped the bombs somewhere near the harbour and were on our way out before the flak opened up. Dadda for God!

We went out to sea on the way home, to avoid the fighters; heading for St Mary's in the Scillies, slowly climbing. Dawn found us still at sea; a lovely morning, the waves an engraving on the brazen glow behind us and sunlight streaming into the cockpit. It was a bit like sailing; I'd once spent a holiday on the Scillies.

Just as we sighted St Mary's, Billy said, 'Junkers about three miles off, dead astern.' And there it was, a little black thing shaped a bit like a tadpole. Such a little thing to spoil a lovely morning . . . But you don't muck about with Junkers 88s, even in daylight. It could overhaul you no faster than a family car, but it had a much tighter turning-circle than we did. Luckily, there was a great patch of cumulus just off St Mary's, and Dadda put us straight into it.

We flew around inside, waiting for the Junkers to need his breakfast. Trouble was, we had to keep turning, to avoid flying out of the cloud again. A certain brightening of the light gave us a bit of warning when to turn, but three times we pushed our nose out, which the wily old Junkers was expecting. But he couldn't outguess Dadda. The first time we came out, the Junkers was miles below us; the second time, he was flying away from us, and the third, he was just crossing our bows. Mad Paul gave him a burst and he could hardly miss. Bits flew off Jerry's port-engine cowling and he sprouted a long white plume of glycol-smoke. *He* knew what it was all about; headed straight for the French coast in a shallow dive. Their rear-gunner even had the nerve to stick up two fingers at us. Paul stuck his right back. Paul wanted to chase him, but Dadda said we'd used up a week's luck already and headed for home, mumbling some uncouth Gaelic ditty under his breath. The Junkers, now far behind, seemed to be roughly holding height; we wished him nothing worse than a ditching, and a pick-up by RAF Rescue.

We landed in high good humour, for once with a good story to tell. The other flight was back, from Osnabrück. S-Sugar was in its pan. We breezed into the debriefing room – and it was just like walking into the Arctic. They just didn't want to know us at all.

It took some time to get anyone to explain what had happened, but apparently a kid called Reaper had been landing after Osnabrück. Now Reaper had once seen some silly bugger overshoot a runway. The effect had been so awful that it had left Reaper with just one ambition in life: never to overshoot a runway himself. So Reaper had his flaps down quicker, his throttles back quicker, his brakes on faster than anybody ever known. They called him the Caterpillar, offered him spare lettuce leaves in the Mess.

Anyway, there was old Caterpillar caterpillaring in when another Wimpey comes in to land straight over the top of him. Its slipstream knocked Caterpillar all over the shop, though luckily he was nearly stopped by then. Then the other Wimpey lands right in front of him, neatly enough, but totally blocking Caterpillar's way to the dispersals. It was S-Sugar. Typical bloody Blackham. He'd even cut his engines. Caterpillar leapt out, apparently, and ran up to S-Sugar like he was going to give Blackham the hiding of his life.

But Groupie in his jeep beats him to it. Just as well. Because there's something funny about S-Sugar. Something odd. The escape-hatches are open and missing, though there's not a speck of damage anywhere on her. Groupie sent Caterpillar away, straight off. Groupie's been flying thirty years; he's got a nose for trouble. So somebody fires a flare to summon the ambulance. Then Groupie goes inside. And the first thing he finds is one dead rear-gunner with a hole in his chest. Poor old Geranium. And there's a thirty-eight service revolver lying just beside him, with one cartridge fired. And not a single bullet-hole in the fuselage . . .

Blackham was one of the few men I knew who carried a revolver on raids, to help his escape if he got shot down.

Of Coade, the front-gunner, Spann, the wireless op, Brennan, the navigator, and Beales, the co-pilot, there was no sign. Groupie umphed a bit at that. They thought Blackham was dead, too, at first. But he wasn't. Just rigid; hands still on the wheel, feet still on the rudder-bar. Staring ahead of him, as if he was still flying. He wouldn't answer when they spoke to him, wouldn't turn his head to look at them. In the end they had to prise his hands off the controls and carry him out on a stretcher. Catatonic schizophrenia, they said later, when he went on sitting and flying S-Sugar in the hospital ward. He's never said a word to anybody from that day to this. And late in the afternoon they phoned to say they'd found the four missing aircrew, buried in a large turnip field near Chelmsford. It seems they'd jumped from too low a height; their parachutes had had no time to open.

Nobody was ever going to know exactly what happened to S-Sugar on the journey home. Her bombs were gone, every single part of her worked to perfection, there wasn't a bullet-hole or a scratch on her. No reason in this world for baling out. So they serviced her and put her back in her pan. Groupie said she could serve as a spare aircraft for any crew whose crate was undergoing repair.

What they should have done was to throw her on to the scrapheap, as we had once thrown away that Messerschmitt propeller-blade. But no one – not even Butcher Harris himself – has the clout to write off a fairly new, totally undamaged plane. And people flew quite regularly – if not cheerfully; never cheerfully – in crates where men had died, where men had been scraped off the seats. But at least we knew what happened to them. Nobody knew what had happened in Blackham's Wimpey.

After that, S-Sugar began to dominate the whole station, as the prop-blade had dominated our barrack-room. Nobody went near her. Shadows seemed to gather inside her cockpit and turrets. She grew to twice the size of any Wimpey on the field. It was the time of the autumn spiders; they spun webs all over her, as they spun them in the hedgerows, as they spun them on the other Wimpeys. Except that flight and servicing and polishing scrubbed the other Wimpeys clean every day. The cobwebs just grew thicker on S-Sugar. The ground-crew sergeant had a strip torn off him by Groupie about it; he swore he cleaned Blackham's Wimpey daily, but nobody believed him. Erks cycling past the pan at night were seen to steer away from it, in a half circle. There were all sorts of rumours in the erks' mess too. Voices had been heard inside it, when there was no one about; crackly intercom voices. Then the WAAFs got hold of the story. Had anybody noticed, they asked, that no birds ever perched on Blackham's Wimpey? Actually, very few birds perched on anybody's Wimpey; they don't make desirable perches, not with so many trees around – but that was the kind of stupid rumour that went around. Not that the aircrews were any better, though they never mentioned it. Aircrew are more superstitious than sailors. They all have mascots: teddy bears, old raggy dolls, umbrellas; won't fly without them, or without peeing on the tail-wheel before they go and after they come back. So it came out afterwards that people had gone to extraordinary lengths not to fly in Blackham's crate. Pilots with defective crates didn't report them, just slipped their ground-crew fivers to work overtime on their personal planes, until they were fit to fly again. More than once there were unexplained fights between crews over job priorities.

Finally, the scandal reached Groupie's ears, and he put his foot down. With all the lack of sympathy that scrambled-egg wallahs are capable of, he picked Reaper to fly S-Sugar on the next op to Tallinn. Reaper's crew immediately put themselves on the chop list. They sat in a tight little group at ops tea, silent, sweating, eyes down, not touching a scrap of their grub. They had spent two days writing letter after letter to say goodbye to their folks back home, giving away their tennis rackets and golf clubs and altering their wills. Nobody could bear to look at them. Most people expected them to crash on take-off, and they damned nearly did.

But they came back. Came back late, made a very wobbly landing, but came back without a scratch. There were a lot of us waiting for them outside the debriefing hut, waiting to break out a bottle of whisky some cheerful type had bought either to drink with them or to their memory. All of us wanted to slap them on the back . . . only, the first bloke who tried it got a punch in the teeth that laid him flat on his face. We left them alone after that.

They answered debriefing in monosyllables. Piece of cake, they said, no fighters, no flak, found the target, easy. But they looked far worse than before they went; more destined for the chop than ever. And as their skipper rose to go, he spat out at the wireless officer, 'Get that bloody intercom seen to!'

Next raid, they had their own plane back, but even that made no difference. They walked out to the truck that took them to the dispersals like – I can't get my tongue round it – like walking corpses. And that time they didn't come back. Oh, and the wireless officer had S-Sugar's intercom checked. It worked perfectly.

Groupie sent out another crew in her. Exactly the same thing happened, with knobs on. Came back in S-Sugar without a mark on them, and crashed their own crate on take-off the following op.

By this time the whole flaming squadron was going down the drain. Groupie had Dadda in for a private talk in his office. I'll say one thing for Dadda; he made a condition with Groupie: he volunteered himself to fly Blackham's Wimpey, he didn't volunteer us. He left us free. Asked for a scratch-crew from round the squadron. Nobody volunteered. Not a single soul, and I don't blame them. So Dadda said he would go on his lonesome.

Matt said he would go with him. Then Mad Paul said you had to die sometime and he'd rather die with Dadda than anybody else. In the end, even I said I would go. The idea of them buying it and me starting all over again with a new crew was unthinkable. Human beings are sheep in the end, aren't they?

It was our twenty-third op.

We get the wink from the control-tower, and Dadda takes off a bit savagely; a tight rein on a strange horse. Is his voice a shade sharper, or is it just the strange intercom? I fiddle with the dials a bit, making no difference, and settle down next to Kit in the black windy tube that's the whole, noisy world.

Only tonight it's the wrong tube; it creaks and flutters in the wrong places. Piercing draughts sneak in from the wrong angles. I stick the nozzle of the heating-hose down my right flying-boot, and it's a marvellous comfort; it's the only thing that's giving me anything; it's the only thing that loves me. I champ my way through a bar of chocolate, before we reach eight thousand feet and we put on oxygen masks. I am glad I can see Kit's face through a gap in his navigator's curtain. It looks calm and thoughtful, as he scribbles steadily on his maps. I love that face more than I love any girl's or filmstar's. It's always there. I could never tell him how I feel, but sometimes he punches me, when we've landed, and I punch him back, and that's it. Still, he'll punch anybody he even vaguely likes. Does he really not give a damn? Does he really think it's all a giggle still, on the twenty-third time? Don't think like that; I need to think he's like that.

As if he senses my stare, even through all his gear, he turns and bats his eyebrows at me, mocking. Behind his mask, I know he's grinning.

'Have you heard the one about the constipated navigator?' He's only three feet away, but his voice on the intercom sounds as far away as the backside of the moon. 'He had to work it out with a pencil.'

Snort from Mad Paul in the front turret.

'Oh ha, ha,' groans Billy.

'Shut up, Kit.' But even Dadda is sniggering.

After the war Kit's going to Oxford, and I'm going back to the True Form shoe shop in Clitheroe. Maybe he'll ask me down for a weekend . . . if there is an after the war.

'Keep that RT down,' says Dadda; his voice *is* sharper, edgier. I fiddle with the knobs. Yes, the glowing dials are a comfort, too; a little glowing city where ants live. Ant palaces, ant cinemas . . .

Blackham's Wimpey is newer than C-Charlie; the wireless-op's seat seems harder-edged and colder than my own. Every crate they send, there's some new modification.

Yes, Kit's jumpy too; makes two course corrections on the way to our wave rendezvous over Cromer. Celebrates too noisily the fact that he's pin-pointed Cromer Pier.

'Shut up, Kit!' snarls Dadda. Normally Kit does us a lot of good on the run-in, but tonight his comedy act's not working. The engine note keeps changing, too; Matt's making heavy weather getting the engines synchronized. And out over the sea, Billy tests his guns; but so often, we think he's seen a night-fighter.

'What the hell . . .?'

'Sorry, Skip. It's this turret. I've got to get used to it.' Blackham, and Blackham alone, blast him, managed to get a four-gun Frazer-Nash turret fitted to *his* Wimpey. Like the Lancs and Halley-bags have. What did he do? Blackmail the gunnery officer? Sleep with the gunnery officer's missus? Wouldn't put anything past Blackham. The rest of us had to put up with two-gun rear-turrets. I think of Blackham, still flying his Wimpey, sitting up in a straight, hard chair in the asylum. They say he pulls all the right invisible levers, and sometimes his flights take twelve hours, from breakfast to supper, then he starts all over again – unless they shoot some drug into him. If they try to stop him flying, he cries. Otherwise, his eyes are like shiny black marbles, they say, staring out of the ward window. Even when he cries.

Stop *thinking* . . .

I stick the heating-hose down my other boot, readjust the RT. What else is there to do? Kit pushes past me, on his way to the cockpit; big as an elephant in his flying-gear. The sheepskin brushes the back of my head; then I feel lonely. Another quick, nervous burst from Billy. Blackham's guns. The guns that did for Gehlen. I remember them all laughing at Gehlen. Now they've gone where Gehlen went . . . God, I'm shaking more than I usually do over the target, and we haven't reached the Belgian coast yet.

Suddenly, light-flak tracer is Morse-coding past the windows. And then rods of pure white light, leaking in through every chink in the fabric. We're caught in a search-light. Then a throbbing through the Wimpey's frame; a light, rhythmic throbbing: our front guns firing.

Blackness and onwards. Paul's voice saying, 'Well, that'll cost him his weekend's pocket money for a new bulb and battery.' He's hit the searchlight, which you can do at three thousand seven hundred feet. Wild cheers all round.

'It was a flak-ship,' says Dadda. 'Converted trawler.'

'Let him go back to catching kippers,' says Billy. Having the last word is a rear-gunner's privilege.

We all feel a lot better.

'Enemy coast ahead,' says Kit. Somehow, it's good to be back in the thick of it.

We'd just crossed the Rhine, spot on course and with a lot of premature rejoicing from Kit, when I began to get a vibration on the RT. You know when you've got your wireless at home tuned in to the Home Service and Reginald Foort is belting away on the theatre organ, and he hits a big note and your set can't take it and gives a kind of blurting rattle? Well, my RT was acting just like that, but much softer at first.

'Tune the RT properly, Gary. Get rid of that mush.' Dadda's voice was suddenly harsh again. I didn't blame him. We were all as twitchy as hell about the intercom, and this noise in it was like a fat fly buzzing inside your head. I moved the tuning-knob, dutifully but without hope. I am never off station.

'Fault in the set, Dadda. Hope it's not going on the blink.'

'I'll *strangle* that RT mechanic . . .'

'Reaper grumbled about this RT,' said Kit, thoughtfully. So had the other crew that bought it. That was all either of them had said, before they got the chop; get the intercom fixed. There was a nasty silence. Everybody was remembering. Nobody had anything to say.

The buzz faded, to the edge of hope, then got slightly louder. I tell you, it was hypnotic; I couldn't pay attention to anything else. Inside, I was praying, pleading with it to go away. I had never heard anything quite like it before. And if the set really went on the blink, we would each of us be alone and helpless, in a howling blizzard of engine noise. Please go away. *Please* go away. Just for tonight. I was talking to the bloody thing; stroking the dials gently, as if the RT was an angry cat that needed placating.

The noise got louder. And not just louder – it was developing a definite rhythm. A bit like a human voice. Like somebody very tiny, shouting to be let out, somewhere deep inside the set. A voice that couldn't yet get out.

'Turn coming up, Dadda,' said Kit. 'Steer one-o-five . . . now.' His voice was too loud, making us jump. God, that infernal buzz *was* like a human voice. If it got any clearer, I'd be able to tell what it was saying . . .

Get a grip, Gary. Or they'll be writing you off as LMF. You'll end up in a bin, like Blackham. Or cleaning the bogs, like the poor ex-gunner who thinks he's a Dornier 217.

'Fifteen minutes to target,' said Kit. 'Hope the PFs aren't pissed again. I get tired of setting the Black Forest on fire.'

For once, nobody laughed at that good old joke.

'Oh frigg off, you miserable lot,' said Kit. 'Where's the flaming funeral?'

He shouldn't have said that. In the stony silence that followed, the idea of a funeral wouldn't go away. Aircrew bodies fished out of burning crates have shrunk so much, they hardly need coffins bigger than shoe boxes.

'Watch the sky,' said Dadda. 'You won't be shot down by a buzz on the intercom.'

'Right,' said Mad Paul.

'Right,' said Billy, a long time after. Billy's reactions were usually as quick as greased lightning. Hell, this whole crew was falling apart.

There wasn't one tiny voice talking inside my RT now; there were two, talking to each other. Oh, electronic mush on the air . . . it was always happening. But not when your RT was properly tuned. I played with the knobs again, pointlessly.

'Five minutes to target,' said Kit. A dim red light was stealing down the black tube of the Wimpey's fuselage from the cockpit windows. We began to bounce under the impact of flak and the slipstream of the other bombers. Berlin coming up.

As I played with the knobs, the voices suddenly became audible, just barely audible.

'Steer two-seven-five. The *Kurier* is five kilometres ahead of you and five hundred metres above.' The voices were talking in German. A night-fighter was being homed-in on its courier, or target.

'Some bugger nattering in German,' said Kit loudly.

'Well, he's not after us,' said Dadda soothingly. 'We're steering one-o-five. Now keep your mind on the run-up.'

So Kit started the old left-left, steady, right-a-bit routine, and for the next five minutes he swamped the German voices. We had other things to worry about.

The darkness after the target is the most beautiful darkness in the world. Dadda checked us one by one. Nobody hurt; no damage as far as we knew. The twin Bristol Hercules droned on blissfully. Take us home, Hercules, great god of antiquity.

But the German voices inside my RT set were still there, louder, quite clear now. If we could hear them, could they hear us? Radio's a funny thing.

'Can you see the *Kurier* yet? He should be a kilometre ahead and fifty metres above you. Still steering two-seven-five. You should see him against the clouds . . .'

'How dense are the clouds, Kit?' I asked.

'What frigging clouds?' said Kit, his head in the astrodome. 'Haven't seen no frigging clouds.'

'It's nothing to do with us,' said Dadda. 'We're steering three-hundred.'

'I'll just test him out on Monica.' Monica is another little bag of tricks that Dadda acquired for me. It has a bulb that lights up when a fighter's tracking you on radar. I switched Monica on, and off again quickly. Monica, lovely girl, said there was nobody on our tail.

But the noise in the RT grew steadily.

'Can you see the *Kurier* yet?'

'Yes, I can see his exhausts. A twin-motored aircraft.'

That made me jump. Wimpeys are the only twin-motors left in the skies over Germany, and there were only thirty or so on this raid.

'He is about half a kilometre ahead, and fifty metres above me. He has not seen me. I will come up under him and give him a tune on my *Schrage Musik.*'

'Some poor soul's for the chop,' said Dadda. The *Schrage Musik* can tear the guts out of a Wimpey before the Wimpey even knows it's being followed.

'Nothing behind *us*,' said Billy. 'It's as clear as day.'

The German voice was now as loud as Billy's own on the intercom. If anything, louder. It might have been inside the plane with us.

'I am a hundred metres behind him now, and twenty metres beneath. My guns are cocked.'

'Anything?' said Dadda.

'Nothing,' said Billy. 'Not a dicky bird behind us.' But the voice had infected us all. I tried Monica again, though I knew it was pointless.

Nothing.

Even Dadda banked the crate left and right, to get a look underneath.

Nothing. But we all shuddered, waiting for the death of the unknown Wimpey. Was it one of our lot? Probably we should never know.

And then a new voice broke in, loud, a shout, full of fear.

'Blackham – corkscrew port – fighter below you!'

'For God's sake, stop shouting, Gary!' said Dadda abruptly. I didn't answer. It *was* my voice; but I hadn't opened my mouth. It was my voice, a month old, coming out of the dark, out of the past. Calling to Blackham, who at this moment was lying in a bed in Colchester mental hospital. And no wonder the night-fighter's voice seemed familiar. It wasn't just a German voice. It was Gehlen's voice. Burnt Gehlen, who we had seen blown in pieces all over Germany.

Then another voice, exultant. 'I got the bastard! I *got* him!' Geranium, dead a month, with a hole in his chest.

'You sure?' Blackham, very Yorkshire-tyke.

'Sure I'm sure. See him burn!' Geranium.

Wild cheers. From Coade, Spann, Brennan and Beales. Dead in a turnip field near Chelmsford.

'Bullfinch Three to Bullfinch. Abandoning aircraft. Port wing on fire. Get the hatch open, Meissner . . .' Gehlen. Dead, burnt Gehlen.

'Shut the bloody RT off, Gary!' Only slowly, I realized it was Dadda talking to me, in the present day. But it was Kit who reached over and turned off the intercom, plunging us into the blessed silence of the engine's roar. When he looked at me, his blue eyes above the oxygen mask were showing white all round. I was shaking from head to foot. My hand shook so much I couldn't undo my mask. Then I was sick, and the spew built up inside it and cascaded over the top. At least it was real and warm and alive.

The next thing I knew, and that, too, came to me very slowly, as in a dream, was that Dadda had put the Wimpey into a hell of a dive. Either that, or we'd been mortally hit. Frankly, I didn't care. I just hung on like a drowning man to a lifebelt. But we pulled out, and I could tell from the movement of the crate that Dadda was ground-hopping. What else could he do to stay alive, with the intercom gone and all his crew, gunners and all, sitting in a paralysed funk? Any night-fighter could have come up behind and stolen our braces and we wouldn't have noticed.

Kit recovered first, as he always did. Bundled past me with a new course for Dadda to fly. That kid was incredible. I sat huddled, cold and still shaking, over the end of the heating-hose; I held it up my jacket, against my crotch. It was a help. I watched the odd trail of tracer flying past the triangular windows, with the innocent wonder of a small child on a railway journey. Nothing came very near. Dadda was giving Jerry very little chance, as usual. Kit came bundling back to his navigator's table and settled to a problem, face very serious. As usual, it was a comfort to watch him. How did people get to have guts like him and Dadda? I must have been at the back of the queue when they were handing out guts.

It was then that I noticed that my RT dials were starting to glow up again. Had I knocked the switch back on, without knowing what I was doing? I reached to switch it off again.

It was switched off.

But the dials continued to glow up. I gave a noiseless moan, as sound filtered into my earphones. Faint cheers.

'Burn, you bastard, burn!'

An incoherent scream from Gehlen. Kit shoved me aside and reached for the off-switch. It was still off. His eyes creased up over his mask. He tried the switch the other way, and the sound of Gehlen's screams grew louder. He turned it to the off position again. Back and forwards he twisted it, back and forwards, faster and faster. But still the voice of Gehlen grew.

'*Mutti, mutti.*'

Kit went berserk then. He grabbed the heavy-duty cables that led to the radio set from the crate's main batteries. Tore them out of their housings on the airframe. Tried to pull them out of the radio with brute force. Then he reached for a pair of rescue shears.

God, he would go up in a blue light! We'd all go up in a

blue light, if the naked ends of the cut wires touched the airframe. Frantically, I tried to wrestle the shears away from him. We were still fighting like maniacs when Dadda separated us. We stood in a triangle, mouthing soundless screams at each other.

Dadda took a rescue hammer and smashed the shut-off RT set. The sparks flew, I can tell you; lucky the hammer had a rubber handle. Silence. The soundless noise of the engines once again closed like a fleecy blanket over our ears. Dadda went back to the cockpit. Kit and I sat and stared at each other. I don't think either of us expected the world to make sense any more. We had got accustomed to living in a nightmare. Kit even produced a flask of coffee and offered me a cup. Coffee in a nightmare. But it still tasted like real coffee – as real as wartime coffee ever is.

We looked at our watches. Kit mimed, 'Half an hour to the Dutch coast.' Then he turned his head to look at a section of the airframe, puzzled. It *was* vibrating oddly, under our backsides, under our ungloved hands. Had we been hit? Had the engines developed trouble, or gone out of synch?

No, it was more like the rhythms of speech. Voices talking. A voice . . .

Suddenly, the voice burst through again, like fire from a hosed-down plane; a fire the firemen thought they had under control.

'Meissner, Ritter! What's holding you up? Are you dead?'

And then the screams, the godawful, burning screams, drowning the noise of the engines, shaking the airframe, tearing at every joint in our bodies. Nothing, nothing left in the world but screaming.

'*Heil Hitler! Sieg Heil, Sieg Heil, Sieg Heil.*'

Kit and I clung together, held on to each other in a barricade of arms, of living flesh and bones. There was nothing else to do. It was all that kept us in existence. That, and the slight

sway of the airframe that told our legs that Dadda, somewhere – Dadda a million miles away – was still flying her.

The screaming gave back a little, like an army preparing for
a fresh assault. Fell to a sobbing.

'*Mutti, mutti.*'

And we felt another movement in the airframe, towards
the tail. Something was moving there, coming slowly towards
us. Kit reached down and pulled aside the curtain round his
navigator's table. I thought it odd that his little table-light was
still shining. I thought it odd that it still existed at all. It
belonged to the real world. He swivelled it towards the tail,
and we both looked.

A man hung there, crucified.

For a moment, for me, the universe rocked on its pivot.
Then I saw it was only Billy the Kid, face-mask, oxygen-hose
and intercom-wires dangling down his front like entrails. His
face was that white sheet again, with three holes burnt in it
now: his eyes and his silently-screaming mouth. His freckles
stood out like blood splashes. And he wasn't crucified; his
arms were braced against the airframe to hold himself up. As
we watched, he drew in a shuddering breath and screamed,
silently, again. He wasn't looking at us; he wasn't looking
anywhere.

Somehow, Kit started towards him. Immediately, Billy let
go of one side of the airframe. He had a hatchet in his hand;
the little hatchet many rear-gunners carry to hack their way
out of the turret, in case of a crash. I wanted to run away. But
a world without Kit was unthinkable, and Kit was still
advancing on Billy.

The hatchet came up; the hatchet came down, on Kit's
head. Fortunately, it struck the upper airframe stringers in its
descent and lost most of its force. Kit grabbed Billy's wrist,
and the next second we were all three struggling on the
Duralumin walkway, a mass of sheepskin and bony, painful

knees, air-hoses and radio-cables. Then we had hold of one of his arms each, and the hatchet was lying at our feet. Kit kicked it from where he lay, and it vanished into the darkness. He grimaced at me; his face-mask had worked loose. Then he nodded up the fuselage to where the rest bed was bolted. Rest bed, ha-ha. Lie-and-groan bed; bleed-your-life-away-and-your-mates-can't-stop-it bed. We got Billy there. He was no longer struggling very hard. His mouth was open and there were long strands of saliva festooning it.

'Hold him down,' Kit mouthed.

I buried my head in Billy's shoulder, wrapped my arms and legs round his and clung on. Now I sensed Dadda was bending over us; I felt better. God, was it Matt doing the ground-hopping? Could Matt really fly this crate like that? I saw the dim glow from the navigator's light glinting on the syringe in Dadda's hand; saw the needle jab into Billy's rounded, straining backside. His shirt and trousers had come apart, and I could see the pale, shining, girlish skin of his back. Billy stiffened at the pain of the needle, then almost immediately began to relax. Next second, there was an agonizing bee-sting in my own backside.

'Hey,' I shouted, 'that's not fair!'

'Sorry,' mouthed Dadda. 'Meant for him.' He pointed at Billy.

I was getting all weak and warm and drowsy, as the morphia took over. I was frightened I would be too weak to hold Billy; but he had had his jab first: he was even drowsier than me.

That was the last I knew. As the terrible screaming started again, I slipped away from it into warm darkness.

When I came round there was no noise but the roar of the engines. Billy the Kid was still out cold, snoring gently. I wondered who had drawn the great big blue marks under his eyes with a pencil. Kit was sitting at his table, still wearily doing his sums. He had no need of his navigator's light now, because sunshine – early, horizontal sunshine – was streaming in through our dirty triangular windows. I made some kind of movement with my arm, and at the third time he saw and came over.

'That noise has stopped,' I mouthed.

'Halfway across the North Sea. Got weaker and weaker. Then it . . . seemed to give up.' He held up five fingers. 'Five minutes to Oadby.'

'Any damage?'

Kit tried to smile, and gave up. The guy with the blue pencil who'd been drawing on Billy's face had been drawing on Kit's too. With a slightly shaky hand, he gave me a flask-top of cold coffee and said, 'No damage. Not a bullet hole. I've checked.'

'We're going to get this home?'

'Dadda says this crate will always get home.'

'What d'you mean?'

But Kit got up and hurried away forward. I heard the note of the engines change, and felt the aircraft tremble as the flaps went down.

Dadda's landing was a perfect three-pointer; never a bounce. We shook Billy awake, got out on to the tarmac and stood round and peed on the tail-wheel. I caught myself wishing our pee was pure sulphuric acid, and that the tail-wheel would dissolve and all S-Sugar with it.

The ground-crew sergeant came up, glancing at wings, tail, everything.

'Good trip?'

'Piece of cake,' said Dadda. He grinned; dried-up saliva wrinkled his lips into strange patterns. 'But the RT needs seeing to. And there's no point in arguing this time – it's smashed to hell.'

Kit actually laughed, even if he couldn't quite finish it.

The debriefing WAAF kept asking me what happened, and I kept on saying, 'Nothing. Piece of cake.'

I came up slowly out of the depths of sleep. The barrack-room was cold and empty. Waking up was a mistake. I'd been happy asleep.

I went to the window. Autumn Fenland mist. Boundary fence. Mud this side and mud beyond, fading away into infinity. Through the fence a few dirty, ragged sheep stared at me, chewing. I despised them for their keen desire to stay alive. Personally, for the first time, I wished to be dead. Oh, not your Pearly Gates opening and St Peter waiting to pin a gong on you. I'd settle for lovely, black-velvety nothing. Not see, not feel, not think. I tried to remember Clitheroe Grammar School, Mum and Dad, and a girl called Betty who wrote to me every week. But the memory of them stayed grey and remote, like photographs in a tattered copy of the *Daily Mail*, blowing around the dispersals.

This, I thought, without much real interest, was the effect of flying in Blackham's Wimpey. This was the huddled, inert state that Reaper's crew had reached, and Edwards', just before they got the chop. In this state, the chop was inevitable. Dieter Gehlen, dead, was claiming more victims than ever. He was deadlier in Blackham's Wimpey than he had ever been in a Junkers 88. To the glory of the Fatherland. And there was no reason why he should not continue to claim victims. Blackham's Wimpey, as Dadda had observed, would always come home. Probably unmarked. It could fly two more whole tours. How Gehlen's ghost managed to keep flak away, and other Jerry night-fighters, God alone knew. But obviously if Blackham's Wimpey bought it, Gehlen's ghost bought it too. And that would not be in the scheme of things . . .

I realized that what I was thinking was quite insane. The only comfort was that we six could huddle in a group, sharing a common insanity. For a bit. Like Reaper's lot; like Edwards' . . . the names tolled in my head like a funeral bell that would not stop.

Why hadn't Reaper reported it? He had, the only way anyone would believe. He had told the ground-crew sergeant to see to the RT. Something was wrong with it. Oh my, was something wrong with it! But what else could Reaper have done? Told Groupie his squadron contained a haunted bomber? That would have got him one of two rewards: either sitting flying a bomber in Colchester mental hospital, like Blackham, or else found to be LMF – lacking in moral fibre – reduced to the rank of AC2 – the lowest rank of erk – and put on cleaning out the bogs on your own station, with all your mates either trying to look you in the face or trying not to look you in the face. That crafty bastard Gehlen had it all taped. My eyes filled with tears of helpless rage. I'd like to *kill* Gehlen, for what he was doing. But that wasn't possible, was it?

The barrack-room door was flung open with a bang, making me jump a yard in the air. I hadn't realized I had that amount of life left in me. It was Kit. He didn't look as if he wished he was dead. Instead, he looked slightly and gleefully insane. I retired into my pit, and he sat on the end of it, swinging his flying-boots.

'You look terrible,' he said.

'I feel terrible.'

'What you reckon to last night, then?'

'Ghost?' I said feebly.

'That bastard knew what he was doing.' He spoke as if Gehlen was a living man. 'He kept on playing himself different ways, for maximum possible effect. Like a dirty old man flashing himself to schoolgirls in the park.'

'How did you *cope*?'

'Oh, we all got in a bunch. I stood behind Dadda's seat, with a hand on Matt's shoulder. Being three together wasn't so bad. It was being alone in the tail that did for poor old Billy.'

'What about Paul in the front?'

'We kept kicking him up the backside. That kept him going. And he popped away at the light flak and searchlights. He didn't hit a thing, but he said it relieved his feelings. He's out there now, fiddling with his motorbike. Doing wheelies up the runway and driving the WO mad.'

'It must help to be mad,' I said. 'How's Billy?'

'No worse than you. He's still with us; just.' He stared out of the window. Then he said, 'That bloody thing didn't scare Dadda at all, you know. All Dadda said was "poor soul". That's what kept me going. That, and the fact that the bastard went on too long. When he was starting to fade, at the end, he sounded like a worn-out gramophone record. I got up enough nerve to walk to the back of the crate after that. You and Billy were curled up like a pair of babes in the wood. I even took a spell in the back turret. Didn't see anything. After that *thing*, what's a Jerry fighter?'

'Well, Gehlen's done for me,' I said. 'Like he did for Reaper and Edwards . . .'

Kit gave me a long hard stare. 'I've got news for you, son. Just had a report on C-Charlie. She's in need of two new engines. Next time we go out, we go out in Blackham's again.'

My world fell in. I didn't think I could have felt worse, but I did. 'I'm not going. It's LMF for me. How do you hold a bog brush?'

'I'll come with you,' said Kit. 'But d'you fancy helping me do something first? I scrounged this out of Paul's bike.' He pulled a stubby, flat whisky bottle out of his sagging tunic pocket. It was full of clear liquid. He let me smell it. Petrol.

'You don't mean—'

'I bloody do! Burn the sod out. If S-Sugar burns up, Gehlen can waste his time haunting the aircraft knacker's yard.'

'You wouldn't dare . . .'

'Try and stop me. What can they do to us, even if they can prove it wasn't a careless fag-end? How about three years in a nice quiet cell?'

'Bliss,' I said, feeling suddenly a whole lot better. 'When?'

'Now,' said Kit. 'Before the ground-crew get to work on her. Dadda brought her home on full boost; there's hardly a cupful of petrol in her. She won't blow up and kill anybody, not unless somebody tries to be a hero with the fire-extinguisher – and *they* can go and hold old Gehlen's hand.' His eyes still had that slightly mad shine, but I went with him. Except for Dadda, we all did, even Billy. Especially Billy.

There seemed not to be a soul about, as we walked to the dispersals across the wet, misty field. But I suppose there are always mechanics working inside the crates, and cosy, nosy buggers looking out of office windows. Which probably accounts for what happened later. You don't normally get a complete aircrew walking out to a crate the morning after an op. S-Sugar loomed up suddenly, as if she were a ghost. From the outside, she looked just like any other Wimpey; that wedgy, faithful-doggy profile. For a moment my mind did a double-take about damaging His Majesty's property. But Blackham's Wimpey didn't really belong to His Majesty any more, though of course His Majesty didn't know it. Matt reached up and pulled down the hatch and ladder. For no particular reason, I climbed in first.

I'd never smelt a bomber the morning after a raid before. Normally, the ground-crew hose them out with disinfectant before we see them again. But this morning S-Sugar smelt as we had left her: petrol, cordite from the guns, a stronger kind of cordite from the German flak, the stench of vomit, the greater stench of the cold, black Elsan, the stink of sweaty socks and another smell that smells like the smell of blue funk. Only a burning Wimpey smells worse, when the crew's still inside.

It was dark, too. Thick dark. Not much pale yellow light showed through the smeared windscreen.

The moment I began to move up the fuselage, I stopped. There was something alive in there. I always know when there's something alive in a place. We have an old grey moggy which hangs round our barrack-room. She's fond of lurking, invisible, among the grey blankets. I always know she's there, somehow, but she always gives me a fright when she jumps out, purring. Now there was something in S-Sugar, and it wasn't a moggy. Much bigger than a moggy. The hair rose on the back of my neck. I tingled all over.

There was a murmur from beyond the rear of the cockpit. The wind was blowing a bit, rocking the Wimpey on her wheels and keening through struts and aerials, but the murmuring was louder than the keening, though half lost in it. It seemed to be coming from somewhere near the RT; softly, rhythmically. I strained to hear it, and the hair on my neck rose afresh. God, this couldn't be happening.

The murmuring was in German . . .

'You have done well, Dieter. You have done very well. Nobody could have asked for more courage and loyalty than you have shown. Now you—'

'What the hell . . .?' Kit, coming up the ladder, bumped into my back. One look at my face silenced him. And Matt and Paul and Billy, as they ascended one by one. We all listened, painfully holding our breath.

'It is time to go now, Dieter. It was terrible, dying, but now you are free. You have done your duty. Go now where there is no more Führer, no more British terror-flyers . . .'.

A ghost talking to itself. No, I just couldn't believe it. My mind was giving way about once an hour these days; almost as regular as breathing.

'Oh, for God's sake, let's get it over with,' said Billy savagely from the back. Bravely, from the back, he began to push Paul and Matt and Kit and me up the fuselage. He mightn't have been so keen, if he'd been in front. I tell you, I was fighting like hell to get back and out of there. Kit was giggling in my ear, wildly.

But in spite of my struggles, I was pushed nearer and nearer the wrecked RT set. There was a too-dark shadow behind the set. I couldn't quite see what it was, because Kit's navigator's curtain was in the way, but I knew damned well that that shadow wasn't shadow, that that shadow shouldn't be there. It looked . . . leathery. Like a crouched airman in leathers.

Then, starting with a near-imperceptible motion, it rose and rose, and looked at us, with a dead-white face under a rounded leather flying-helmet.

I shut my eyes and screamed again. My throat was already sore with screaming. A very solid hand reached out towards me, grabbed my arm.

'Steady, Gary,' said Dadda.

He had been there almost since we landed, seven hours before. Just got debriefed, then went to his billet to fetch a couple of things and straight back into the stinking bowels of S-Sugar. He clutched the few things against his flying-jacket now, with one hand. A fair-sized black book, and what looked like a string of fat black beads, with a little black cross on one end. 'Relics of Maynooth,' he said, with a wry, weary grin.

'I thought you'd be back,' he added. 'And that will be petrol in the whisky bottle, young Kit? I knew I didn't have all that much time.' Kit had the grace to gape.

'Give me that bottle, Kit.'

'I'm going to bloody do it!' said Kit, very defiant.

'No, you're not,' said Dadda. 'I'm going to do it. I'm skipper.' Kit was so shocked, he forgot to argue.

Dadda turned and looked at the smashed RT set. 'I've tried to persuade him to go.' He sighed. 'But he's very young, and very proud, and very brave, and, sadly, very much in love with his beloved Führer. I don't think I've done any good, with all my talking.'

'Has he said anything?' asked Billy, curious.

'No,' said Dadda. 'Nothing at all. It's been me doing all the talking. Now let me have one more go, like good lads. Get outside and wait for me. And stand well back.' He began to kick and scrape together on the walkway the debris of the night: greaseproof paper from the corned beef sandwiches, discarded maps and navigational instructions, my own Morse-code pad. Then, thoughtfully, he unscrewed the whisky bottle and poured out the clear liquid.

The sharp, dangerous smell of petrol filled our nostrils.

We bundled out, suddenly chattering like schoolboys on Bonfire Night, full of a sick sense of a treat to come. There were a few erks cycling past through the thinning mist, and some ground-crew kicking their heels under A-Able in the next pan. That sobered us. There were more people about than we'd thought. We spotted Dadda's old thirty-hundred-weight parked to one side of the perimeter track, and hung about there. A ground-crew WO approached with steady ringing tread.

'What are you lot on?'

We shuffled. Aircrew-sergeant's stripes, to a ground-crew WO, are as thin as the toilet paper they're printed on. And it *was* unusual for an aircrew to go out to a Wimpey, the morning after an op. The ground-crew think they own the bloody crates; they only lend them to us for ops, and they even make us feel guilty when we bend them.

'Waiting for our skipper,' said Kit humbly. 'He's giving us a lift.'

'You lot get in our hair,' grumbled the WO. 'We've got a lot to do, you know.' He kept looking at us; he wasn't going to go away. He could sense the excitement bubbling up inside us; suspected some sort of practical joke.

'Flight-lieutenant Townsend's lot, are you?'

'Yeah,' said Kit, so quiet you could hardly hear him.

Dadda emerged down the ladder, in a rush occasioned by the respect we all have for the effects of burning petrol. He spotted the WO instantly, and walked across, long-boned and relaxed. He was smoking a fresh fag; tipped the ash on to the WO's shining toecaps, as if he wanted him to notice. The WO backed off, surreptitiously wiping each ash-covered toecap in turn on the back of the other trouser leg.

'You shouldn't be smoking aboard an aircraft, sir,' he said, half cringing, half bad-tempered. Still uneasy.

'I shouldn't be alive at all,' said Dadda. A bit of the old aircrew boast, putting ground-crew in its proper place. 'Sorry. One forgets about the smoking. C'mon, gang, let's go and find some ham-and-eggs.' He opened the door of the thirty-hundredweight so casually that I wondered whether he'd lost his nerve and scrubbed the whole thing. We turned, to pile in the back.

Behind us, the WO called out, 'Hey!' Softly, to himself.

We swung round, and saw the leaping red flicker in the Wimpey's cockpit. Saw the first bit of fabric crinkle and blister and peel back from the airframe. Saw the first red serpent of flame lick its way upwards, eating into the mist overhead.

'Hey!' the WO shouted again, and began to run towards S-Sugar. But doped fabric burns fast. Halfway there he changed his mind and stood stupidly, shielding his face with his hand against the heat. A few more seconds and the whole front end of the crate was going up.

People came running from all directions; it seemed like everybody on the whole airfield. In the distance, the warning sound of ambulance and fire engine. But some way off the fire engine stalled; they said afterwards the plugs oiled up . . .

Everyone stood and gaped. Especially when the voice started. The German voice, right here in the middle of an English airfield. Leutnant Dieter Gehlen, having his last fine careless rapture. And he might have claimed his last victims then, because several erks made crazy attempts at rescue. But the Wimpey was too far gone, aflame from nose to tail. And the voice grew so loud, it echoed round the mist-filled airfield; more than human, essentially the voice from a radio, distorted and full of static crackle.

'Bullfinch Three to Bullfinch . . . port wing on fire. Get the hatch open, Meissner . . .'

They backed away as the crate turned into a torch in which nothing human could have lived. Yet the voice still grew louder and louder.

'*Heil Hitler! Sieg Heil!*'

Then the screaming; terrible, familiar.

'What is it?' shouted the WO, to no one in particular. 'My God, what *is* it?'

An aircraft's fabric doesn't take long to burn through. Within another minute, S-Sugar was a blackened skeleton, filled with black blobs. There was no big bang. The front guns fired two rounds as the heat reached them; then the four guns in the tail – fortunately aimed only at the earth bank of the dispersal-pan – got off a long burst all on their own. There were individual flame-ups of flares and glycol; then, for a short time, the near-empty petrol tanks kept us lively.

And still the German voice bellowed on, out of the

blackened skeleton. The ghost of Dieter Gehlen, born in flame, was consumed in flame. If the life of a happy man flickers like a candle for seventy years and gutters out, the short life of Dieter Gehlen burned out like a rocket. All that assembled crowd, the aircrew especially, knew then what had done for Blackham and Reaper and Edwards. But I don't think that ground-crew WO knows to this day.

At last, silence. He was gone. All that guts, all that energy, all that faith in an evil, unworthy cause. All that hatred of the *Britische Terrorflieger*. I like to think he baled out before the bitter end, and landed at the Pearly Gates, and got a halo for mistaken effort. But I doubt it.

'They shouldn't have laughed at him,' said Dadda softly, to himself. 'They shouldn't have laughed at him.'

At this point old Groupie turned up in his jeep. He asked a few questions, didn't bother waiting for the answers and had our whole crew placed under close arrest. There was a sort of low rumble from the assembled aircrews that suggested, even to Groupie, that he hadn't particularly improved the shining hour.

We were questioned closely. Dadda admitted to lighting a fresh fag from a dog-end inside the crate, and maybe being a bit careless when he disposed of the dog-end. But there was too much flak flying round the station for Groupie not to know that something was up. Over the next twelve hours we were frantically marched here and there, which was a bit rough, though nothing like as bad as doing an op. Especially as every time we went out, we got more cheers than the last time. And we heard that Groupie was having the same experience, only with boos and catcalls.

Then Groupie brought in all kinds of guys to ask us questions; the coldest-smiling top brass RAF police I'd ever seen. If they're *that* terrifying, why aren't they out in North Africa, scaring the Germans? There were also technical experts, pretty in well-pressed blues, and a couple of civvies who I think were trick-cyclists. We stuck to our story: nothing. Dadda stuck to his fag-end. We spent a lot of time reading old comics and polishing kit that hadn't been polished since we got there. Meanwhile, the cheering and jeering got worse, and the adjutant ill-advisedly uttered the word 'mutiny'.

Groupie had us in one last time, late that night, and began going on about LMF. Dadda looked at him in a way even Groupie found hard to take. They went on staring and staring at each other till the WAAF stenographer dropped her pencil. Then Dadda offered to prove that his crew did not lack moral fibre. In the morning, he said, we would do a solo raid up the Pas de Calais, strafing gun-sites from zero feet. If Groupie would care to accompany us, he would have the chance to observe personally if the crew of C-Charlie lacked moral fibre. It would have been pure suicide, of course. But as Groupie fixed his gimlet eyes on each of us, we gazed right back and nodded in turn. I even managed to stop myself swallowing.

We had Groupie over a barrel. He hadn't been expecting this. And too many people were there to hear our offer, including the WAAF, whose eyes were standing out like chapel hat-pegs. Threaten as he might, news of it would be all over the base by morning. Mind you, I wouldn't want to do Groupie an injustice. He'd have come up the Pas de Calais with us, if it would have done the war effort any good. But I think he saw then that we were another kind of problem. He rubbed out *LMF* after our names, and put in *Crazy* instead. The Crazies do exist; we'd met them. There was one air engineer I came across in London on leave who'd done four tours in Lancs. He would lie on his bed and try to trim his toenails with a .38 revolver. Crazies are hooked on destruction. They're clean over the horizon, and never coming back.

Groupie went off into his private sanctum and closed the door and got on the blower, to somebody you could tell didn't welcome being woken up. Maybe it was Butcher Harris on his bath night. They say old Butcher plays with bombs in his bath, like admirals play with boats. We couldn't even hear Groupie's end of the conversation properly, but the tone was 'How the hell do I get out of this one?' Then Butcher, or whoever it was, had a bright idea. You could tell that from the sudden change in Groupie's tone. A moment later he came out and told Dadda to take his crew and every last bit of their kit and possessions, and load them into C-Charlie and depart at crack of dawn. Dadda asked what about C-Charlie's overdue engine-overhaul? Dadda was told where he could stuff C-Charlie's overhaul. Or rather, it would be done after arrival at the new station. The expression on Groupie's face implied he wouldn't break his heart if C-Charlie crashed on the way.

Dadda asked where he was to fly us to. Groupie told him St Mawgan, in Cornwall.

'Long-range attack on Tokyo via Mexico City,' muttered Kit to me. Groupie froze him with a look, but said nothing. We were officially Crazies now, and no longer under his command. All he wanted was to see the back of us.

We reached our billet feeling slightly drunk, and began throwing stuff into our kitbags; throwing stuff at each other. Billy proved what a rotten shot he really was by heaving a boot through the window. We all thought that was an excellent idea, and joined in. When there were no barrack-room windows left (thank God it was only September) and no mirror either (we'd all have liked seven years' bad luck, after months of the prospect of less than seven hours), we sat on our beds and talked.

'What's St Mawgan?' asked Paul, taking a breather from working out how to get his motorbike inside C-Charlie.

'Probably missions of an extra-hazardous nature,' said Matt solemnly, and hiccuped.

'Like delivering milk to the *Tirpitz* and picking up the empties,' said Kit.

Just then we heard the thirty-hundredweight pull up outside. We loaded up, including the motorbike. It was starting to get light and we espied an RAF policeman leading a dog on a bit of string towards the small-arms firing range. It was a little runt of an Alsatian thing, with ears that were still floppy. We all knew where it was going, and so did the dog. Its head was down and its tail drooped. Aircrew aren't supposed to keep pets, but they do. They ask their mates to take them over, if they get the chop. But if their mates get the chop as well . . . The police were always taking dogs up to the firing range, with a shovel in the other hand. Anyway, Kit makes for this policeman with terrible speed, and we all take after him like the clappers. Including Dadda, who is quietly swearing to himself. The policeman pulls up, a look of amazement and then of acute distress on his face.

'I don't like you,' says Kit. 'I don't like you at all. I would not wish to have your company. I would rather have the company of that dog.'

'I'm only obeying orders,' said the policeman, licking his lips.

'So is Heinrich Himmler,' says Kit, rather unreasonably I thought. I mean, Himmler gets far more overtime pay than an RAF policeman. Kit holds out his hand. 'That's *my* dog.'

'Who says?'

'We do,' we all chorused. He looked from one to the other of us, bewildered. It's rather fun being an official Crazy.

'Give him the dog, Corporal,' says Dadda, very crisp and RAF.

'Yessir,' says the policeman, standing to attention with

relief and giving a very fine salute. Oh to be a single-celled animal . . . We bundle back into the truck.

'What you going to call him, Kit?'

'Dieter. Leutnant Dieter Ernst Gehlen. But Dieter for short. He's one of the crew now. He buys it, we all buy it. He lives, we all live. He flies. Every damned op. What the hell has he got to lose? If he wasn't here with us, he'd be dead by now. Pure profit. He's gained five minutes' life already.' He fondled Dieter's ears affectionately, and Dieter licked his face with some enthusiasm. He'd lost his chop-list look already.

At precisely o-four-thirty-five hours, C-Charlie got clearance for take-off. With a bomb load of fifteen kitbags, one BSA motorbike and one happy dog. Nobody was supposed to know we were going, but a lot turned out to see us off.

Dadda flew down to St Mawgan at a very moderate height and a very moderate speed. I don't think he wanted to risk straining the crate's engines. It was funny, starting out with the sun coming up over our shoulders.

'We've gone west at last,' said Kit. 'So this is heaven?'

'Looks more like Slough,' said Paul.

'Not the Slough of Despond?' Kit was in a daft mood. He had nothing to do; navigationally, it was a trip round the bay. We all gawped like trippers at a countryside of mist and hill, cornfields turning pink in the sunrise, with reaping machines and hay carts left any-old-how overnight. A countryside we would never have to bomb; where early farmhands looked up at us once and pedalled on. Where we weren't *Terrorflieger*.

Soon the pale blue of the Bristol Channel crawled over the horizon, to join the English Channel in sharpening the land to a pencil-point. Devon and Cornwall narrowed and narrowed; the sea gathered in as if, if not to welcome us, at least to look us over. The slice of atmosphere spilling into the

Wimpey smelt cleanly of ocean and seaweed. We took a crafty look at St Mawgan from the air. It had the solid brick buildings of a permanent station; no more tents and Nissen huts. And even from up aloft you could see traces of RAF bullshit: whitewashed patterns of stone round a guardroom; what would be a flowerbed again in the spring. I turned up the RT, so Dadda could speak to the control-tower. Tower, a rich, fruity voice, finished up by saying, 'You've chosen the right day to arrive. Mutton chops for lunch and the Saturday hop.'

Silence. We were all knocked silly by the idea of a regular Saturday hop. Saturday night was the Butcher's favourite time for the Happy Valley, the Ruhr that is.

'This place sounds like bloody Butlin's,' Kit blurted out.

'Watch your tongue, Sergeant,' said Dadda, more RAF than I'd ever heard him.

'I heard that,' said the fruity voice, not at all put out.

That Saturday hop was quite a thing. A sea of floral dresses; the smell of face powder and the swish of silk stockings. Not a bad band, either: three corporals and three LACs and a nice semi-professional touch, even if the music was a bit out of date; provincial. Most of us just sat and watched anyway, and breathed in the females, though Billy the Kid got involved with a red-haired WAAF with an amazing pair of Bristols. And Paul found a guy who owned a motorbike.

I just kept watching the faces. There were a lot of steady couples, staid, steady couples. Nobody living it up, kicking the place apart, or twitching. The aircrew looked hard-worked, but they had the ruddy look of fishermen or shepherds. Many were quite solid round the middle; if bombers make your guts screw up, the boredom of Coastal Command makes you nibble. They looked middle-aged; quite a number had balding heads. But none of them looked as if he was on the chop-list.

It was so hot and flowery-smelling, I fell asleep twice. But I wouldn't go to bed. I was too busy absorbing the possibility of having some sort of future.

And that's the way it's been, the last ten months. It's not a soft life in Coastal. Try crawling out of your bed in a five a.m. blizzard and trying to keep your perspex frost-free with your heating-hose and fingernails. And our lot have lost three crews in ten months. We often wonder what happened to them. Maybe they met one of those Junkers that get into the north end of the bay; maybe they met a wind that read 120 knots on their API. But that's the point: we have time to sit and wonder what happened to them, and that's quite a luxury. We sometimes stay in the air for thirteen hours at a stretch with extra-load tanks, and that's a lot of time to wonder, while you're watching the radar screen for the tiny blip that means a U-boat schnorkelling.

Meanwhile, we too have turned into fishermen and shepherds. We've dropped plenty of depth-charges, of course, but as far as we know killed nowt but blossoming white circles of belly-up fish. We met a U-boat once, on the surface off the Skellig, when we were coming home with no depth-charges left. Paul exchanged a few words with it, and it left the scene of the crime rapidly. We weren't all that bothered.

Otherwise, we see a lot of sunrises and sunsets from high up, and study the flight of birds. A storm-petrel came through the windscreen once, and wrapped itself round Dadda's neck. Paul reckoned it had been trained by the Japs in kamikaze tactics. We had it stuffed for the billet mantelpiece. And we fly round in big circles and little circles, just like herring-gulls, but a bloody sight colder. But when we leave a convoy and their Aldis winks 'thank you', we feel a bit warmer.

Everything says we're going to finish the war here; the forgotten army. They've taken away Tinsel and the H2S. Dadda wouldn't let them pinch Monica. They've covered our black paint with a lovely coat of Coastal white, with two black bands round the fuselage. And we haven't burnt any more crates. Dieter is great; he's not grown much, but he's put on weight and got this glossy, all-black coat that makes him look a proper Nazi. Which is a laugh, because he'll lie down for anybody to tickle his belly. He likes riding in the front gun-turret, slobbering over Paul with excitement. He flies every op; Coastal understand about mascots; they're nearly all ex-bomber anyway.

Oh, and we've got this new game. Dadda disclosed that his family have a ruined castle and estate at a place in Eire called Castletownsend. We're all going to live there after the war, as gamekeepers and illicit whiskey-distillers and things. He did a zero-feet raid on the Republic last month, to show us the castle from the air. The Irish authorities complained, but Dadda just told the Wingco he had an Irish passport. I don't know if any of Dadda's story is true, but it helps to pass the time.

Yes, we get a lot of time to think, in Coastal. Think about the old squadron; all new faces by now, nobody left who remembers the end of Dieter Gehlen. Think about all the English ex-schoolgirls filling bombs till their backs ache, all the German schoolgirls making shells. Think about the guts of German mothers in Hamburg, sheltering their kids with their own bodies from the fire-typhoon we started. Think about the craftsmen's skill in a Rolls-Royce Merlin, and a German medieval cathedral. All those people with all that guts, and our top brass are just turning them all into one great big rubbish tip that's slowly covering Europe. While we watch seagulls.

I sometimes think, towards the end of a thirteen-hour flight, that we died after all, that we're in some kind of peaceful grey Valhalla where good little aircrews go. But where are the rest? Blackham and Reaper and Edwards? And Dieter Gehlen?

Don't ask me. It's May 1944, and I think I've got the little WAAF in the radio stores interested.

Two more pints, please, George.

FRED, ALICE AND AUNTY LOU

Angela Burscombe and Biddy Stevenson were friends. They shared a flat, and many mistook them for sisters, because they were both big, brunette girls with bright eyes and fond of a giggle. But they'd only met at the primary school where they taught, and where new kids had a lot of trouble telling them apart. They were friends because they could tell each other most things, but not everything, and they didn't live in each other's pockets. They got out and lived it up.

They were the sort that any sensible man will immediately pursue. As a result, they soon married; and they married two of Flamborough's coming men, but rather older than themselves. Angela married Peter Wingfield, the writer, and Biddy married Roger Trembling, who was big in computers. The flat-partnership broke up, but the friendship remained. They saw each other, sensibly, twice a week for coffee and chat, and no more.

There might have been no trouble, if they hadn't both enjoyed their marriages. Unfortunately they thought that since they enjoyed their husbands so much, the husbands must inevitably enjoy each other too. The two couples got into the habit of dining at each other's houses on alternate weeks.

Equally unfortunately, the husbands had known each other at Flamborough Grammar, and cordially loathed each other.

There was a clash of husbandly life-styles. Peter Wingfield was a genial shambles, with balding head and a great mat of beard that totally hid any collar and tie, in the manner of W. G. Grace. When he got stuck with his writing, he fled to the kitchen and savagely attacked new wholemeal loaves and half-pounds of butter. When he was writing well, he lit fag after fag, and even though he only took one puff of each, and left the rest to smoulder in the ashtray, he wheezed a bit when he ran. And, thanks to the wholemeal bread, he had a paunch; not much of a paunch, but a paunch. Enough for Roger Trembling to poke, saying:

'Why don't you take up squash and get yourself back into shape?'

Angela always responded loyally, 'I like his shape. He's lovely as he is. Leave him alone.' But there was a hint of wistfulness in her voice that was acid and asps to the soul of Peter.

Roger Trembling played squash three times a week, skied every February in Austria, and often tried to pluck folds of flesh off his braced stomach. He also invited Angela to do it. It seemed to Angela that Roger's stomach was so lean and hard that she never got more off it than a fold of his immaculate white shirt.

Peter dressed like a shambles too. He had a wardrobe full of new suits, which Angela got him to buy whenever he won some kind of literary prize. Peter dutifully wore them once, then went back to the old corduroy jacket with beer stains that he had worn at college. On the other hand, Roger had his hair trimmed every week, and often wore an immaculate blazer. Privately, Peter referred to him as 'Action Man'.

Their homes were also different. Peter had bought a rambling Edwardian semi-mansion with attics and Virginia creeper. He had a keen eye for antiques, but never worried if a thing fitted in, or was too big, as long as it was genuine and good. He also had five cats, which he brought up by the permissive method. On one memorable occasion, Roger put his foot into a piece of mislaid cat dirt, while admiring a Chippendale chair. Peter was also keen on gardens, but loved plants so much that he could never bear to pull up a promising weed; especially after he got 'into' Findhorn literature and flower-fairies. Privately, Roger referred to the Wingfield household as 'the Haunted Mansion' or more simply as 'the Jungle'.

The Trembling house, on the other hand, was flat-roofed, five-bedroomed and stood starkly amidst acres of lawn that would not have shamed Wimbledon. It was known to the Wingfields as 'Mission Control'. The furniture was all stainless steel and teak, full of edges and sharp corners that dug you cruelly in the thigh unless you were stone cold sober. Peter would frequently amble about for minutes on end, and, when finally asked sharply what was the matter, would complain he was looking for a comfortable place to sit.

It was Angela and Biddy's fault, more than they knew. Each babbled happily to the other about her husband's peculiarities; Roger had bought a book in German on erotic lovemaking, three inches thick, which he kept by the bedside and sometimes consulted; Peter had gone shopping with Angela and absent-mindedly picked up the coal scuttle instead of the shopping basket, and had been halfway round the shops before he noticed. These stories were gleefully received and stored up by the husbands as evidence of each other's lunacy.

Every time they dined together, each husband in turn lay in wait for the other with a test. Peter would thrust some cob-webbed or soil-covered object under Roger's nose, and say:

'What do you make of that?'

Roger always said, 'Prehistoric piss pot.' But after the first time it never got a laugh.

Roger would retaliate by attacking Peter with some new wonder of science dragged home specially from the research labs. One was a mini-chipped device for taking blood pressure from fingertips. Peter's blood pressure was alarmingly normal.

But the worst time was when Roger brought home a chess-playing computer of advanced design. Peter had been a reasonable player at school; he now played the computer with such brilliant, savage idiocy that it began to blink green distress signals. Roger fiddled with it, but it seemed Peter had actually done it some kind of harm. It also turned out that Roger had no permission to borrow it in the first place.

'You're just not *normal*,' snarled Roger, as they sat down to the melon.

'You're so normal it's abnormal,' said Peter, swigging at the red wine in a happy, sweating flush.

Roger began discussing a new computer which was being programmed to write novels, having been fed all the basic thought patterns of Conrad, Dostoevsky, Proust and Ian Fleming. Roger implied that in five years Peter would not only look like Neanderthal man, but be equally obsolescent.

It was not a happy meal.

It was when they got home, though, that Angela said the fatal thing. It was only ten days to Christmas, and she made the unfortunate remark that they had not yet sent Roger and Biddy a Christmas card. And there were none left in the house.

'Don't worry, love. I'll see to it tomorrow – I've got to go into town.'

Angela looked at him sharply. It was not like him to be helpful in small matters, like Christmas cards. And he had a look of schoolboy glee on his face she'd learnt to mistrust. But she was busy with Christmas, and she didn't want to upset him any more, after the bashing Roger had given him. Probably he'd forget; he usually did with small things, and then she could safely do it herself.

But the next evening, over tea, when she asked him, he said:

'Oh, yes, I've done that. Consider it done. Worry your head no more, fair lady. Actually, I sent them two.'

Again she looked at him sharply, but he only smiled.

'Wait and see. Wait and see.'

They dined at Mission Control the day after Boxing Day. Angela spent a frantic first half-hour, Martini in hand, admiring and surreptitiously looking inside all Roger's three hundred Christmas cards. Certainly, she thought, the atmosphere *seemed* cordial enough. Peter couldn't have done anything too dreadful.

'Your card was *most* unusual,' called Biddy, head round the kitchen door.

Angela broke out in a cold sweat and slopped Martini down a swollen green-and-purple version of the Three Wise Men that made them look like week-old corpses. Biddy hurried across, wiping floury hands on her apron, and held up a positively huge Rembrandt card.

'It was sweet of Peter; it must have cost the earth – we're thinking of having it framed after Christmas.'

Even Roger beamed. Peter said:

'Trying to educate the New Illiterate. It'll be some years before the mini-chip gets round to Rembrandt.'

'Oh, yes, *some* years,' said Roger, almost jovially. Full of Christmas spirit. A happy moment, everybody smiling, like the cover of a glossy gift catalogue.

Then Roger's smooth white brow creased in a frown. 'Not like the *other* thing,' he said. He took a deep gulp of Martini. 'Show them, Biddy.'

Biddy searched carefully among the back ranks of cards for something small and hidden. 'I didn't like not to put it up at all. I mean, whoever they are, they meant well. And it is

Christmas . . .' She fished it up and held it out to Angela.

It was a horrid little card, a mean little card. The cheapest and nastiest little card Angela had ever seen. Holly, robins and bells, and even carol-singers, all crammed into a three-inch square, smudgily printed in viciously dull shades of black and green.

'Look inside,' said Roger, with thin disgust in his voice. Angela looked. It said:

From Fred, Alice and Aunty Lou

'Well?' asked Angela.

'We don't know any Fred, Alice or Aunty Lou,' said Biddy. 'And look what else they've written.'

Angela looked.

Ever so nice to see you at Blackpool this summer. Will call between Christmas and New Year.

'We've never been to Blackpool in our lives,' screeched Roger. Well, it was nearly a screech anyway.

'Perhaps it came to the wrong house,' said Angela. 'Perhaps it wasn't meant for you, and you opened it by mistake.'

'I thought of that,' said Roger. 'No way. I looked through the dustbin till I found the envelope. It was addressed to us all right.'

'It was right at the bottom of the bin. He was out there till after midnight, looking. By torchlight. I went to bed in the end and left him to it. Then he brings this stinking little envelope up to the bedroom and drops tea leaves all over the white bedspread. Acting like he'd found the crown jewels . . .'

'Must have been good exercise for you, old man,' said Peter. 'Keep you in shape.'

Angela silenced him with a look. But Roger did not even seem to have noticed the jibe. He blundered on.

'But who are they? Who *are* they?'

Peter took the card from Angela, and assumed a heavily judicious air.

'Well, speaking as a non-computer, a mere scribbler, I would say they are definitely not *our* sort of people.'

Roger flinched. Peter continued.

'Definitely your workers, these. About fifty years old, I'd say; Fred and Alice, that is. I can almost see them. Fred in a cardigan, unbuttoned to let his paunch hang out. Shirt done up, but no tie. Balding, and so many wrinkles on his forehead, he could screw his hat on. Fond of his pint. Laughs at his own jokes. Alice . . . Alice is a bit more difficult. Tight-permed, blue-rinsed hair. Blue fly-away spectacles. Big handbag full of snaps of Darren and Tracy and the other grandchildren. As for Aunty Lou . . . thick, grey, lisle stockings and a *smell* . . .'

Angela could have screamed. That was exactly as she had seen them too. Was Peter a magician? Or was she just used to living with him, knowing the way his mind worked? He was certainly having a terrible effect on Roger; Roger had turned quite green around the gills. But why; why was he reacting so strongly? Then she had a vision. Roger and Biddy with their parties between Christmas and New Year, almost perpetual parties . . . bosses, colleagues – smart parties. And then a ring on the bell and . . . in walk Fred, Alice and Aunty Lou. Instant disaster.

Only it wasn't going to happen. Because Fred, Alice and Aunty Lou were inside her own husband's head. This was the second card he'd sent. She opened her mouth to spill the beans. Then she looked at Peter. And he firmly shook his head at her, with a look that froze up her mouth.

'If they come near here,' said Roger desperately, 'I'll call the police.'

'Oh, darling, you can't,' wailed Biddy. 'It's Christmas . . .'

She didn't tackle him about it until they were drinking their Horlicks. He was sitting in the bedroom chair, wearing a large-checked dressing gown that he must have had since he was fourteen; both the tassels of the cord had unravelled, and one elbow was paling into a hole. She had twice bought him nice new dressing gowns; he had never worn either. But he looked reassuringly harmless in this one; still a fourteen-year-old, wearing a false beard for a joke. Or like an amiable dancing bear.

She decided on the casual approach. 'That Christmas card. What a scream. Roger's face! I could have died. How did you fake the writing?'

It had been a mean, crabbed script, totally unlike Peter's wild, generous hand.

He looked at her; she couldn't read the expression in his eyes.

'*I* didn't fake any writing.'

'You got someone to write it for you. Go on, *admit* it. That was the second card you sent them.'

He took a deep swig of Horlicks, and stroked the brindled cat on his knee. The brindle pushed her cheek against his face enthusiastically; all the cats adored him; queued up, had fights to sit on his knee.

He looked at her. 'Drop it, Angel. It's got nothing to do with *you*.'

She still felt absolutely safe with him, because she knew he loved her. But it suddenly struck her that he did not love everybody. That perhaps not everybody was as safe as she was . . .

The second card came in the middle of January. From Blackpool. It said:

Just having a few days winter break. Weather is quite bracing. Wish you were here. Will call soon.

    Love,
        Fred, Alice and Aunty Lou

The front was a picture of Blackpool Prom., with a row of hotels. One window of one of the hotels was marked with an *X* in blue biro.

'You could check on that,' suggested Peter.

'I did,' said Roger. 'I phoned. They were registered. Mr and Mrs F. Brown. And a Mrs Louise Brown, booked into an adjoining room. I drove up there – and I wish I hadn't. I saw the register; the hotel staff thought I was barmy. It was the same handwriting – I took a photocopy for the police. The address they gave was 26 Brannen Street, Flamborough.'

'And?' asked Peter.

'The whole of Brannen Street is derelict – empty. They're demolishing it next week to build a factory for the Japs.'

'Didn't you make enquiries?'

'No one to ask.'

'Get any description from the hotel staff?'

'It was one of those cheap, pensioner block-bookings. They couldn't remember a thing.'

'So you wished you hadn't gone,' Peter said gently.

'Oh, that's not why I wished I hadn't gone,' replied Roger grimly. 'On the way home down the motorway, a bloody juggernaut crossed the central reservation and came straight at me. I shouldn't be alive. The Jag's a write-off.'

There was a long pause, then, before Biddy asked Peter how the latest book was going.

Angela and Biddy were sitting in the kitchen of Mission Control having coffee. It dawned on Angela after half an hour that, every so often, Biddy was giving a surreptitious sniff.

'Got a cold coming?' asked Angela sympathetically. Biddy did look rather under the weather.

'No, why?' asked Biddy with a manufactured burst of brightness.

'You keep sniffing.'

'There seems to be a smell,' said Biddy. 'Can you smell anything?'

Angela sniffed in turn. The idea of *any* smell in Mission Control was almost sacrilege. There were things for dealing with smoke and fumes (in their little white containers like knights' helmets), not just in the kitchen and loo, but in every room. Angela had noticed that since her marriage, Biddy too had gone completely odourless, like water with the faintest hint of pine. Now, in the deodorized bleakness of Mission Control, there *was* a faint odour, obvious as a distant lighthouse at sea on a dark night.

'Yes, I *can* smell something,' said Angela.

'I've changed all the air-fresheners twice this week,' said Biddy fretfully. 'But they don't seem to be working. I couldn't get Roger to bed until two o'clock this morning. He kept wandering round and round, snatching open doors and looking under cushions over and over again, like a mad thing. Threatening to call the police.'

'Why, for heaven's sake?'

Biddy shrugged despairingly. 'That smell you can smell – what's it a smell *of*?'

Angela drew in deeply through her finely-flaring nostrils. Finally she said, 'An old lady. Mints and . . . and . . .'

Biddy nodded grimly.

'But surely you've had old people here?' The Jungle saw a fair number of elderly relatives from time to time, including Peter's father, who smoked a pipe that smelled like the corporation incinerator.

'Never a one,' said Biddy. 'We go to them – when we have

to – twice a year. I miss my gran a lot. Roger can't stand old people.'

'Oh.' Angela sniffed again. She was rather proud of her sense of smell. She got up and moved around the room.

'Not you as well,' protested Biddy, weakly. But Angela was hot on the scent, keen as a schoolgirl with a new game.

'It seems to be coming more from the lounge.' On and on she went, quite lost to the world, giving a grand impression of Sherlock Holmes' bloodhound, finally going down on her knees and sticking her bottom in the air.

'Eureka!' She pulled back one of the cubic cushions on the cubic settee, pushed her hand down the crack at the back and said, 'I think there's something here.' Then she pulled out a tiny tangle of cloth and metal with sharp points.

It was a wretched piece of knitting; the beginnings of a scarf, grey and maroon. Angela heard an odd sound behind her, and looked up to see Biddy, face white, eyes staring and knuckles held to her mouth. She grabbed her arm. 'What is it, love, what is it?'

'Smell it,' ordered Biddy. Angela did; the aroma of old woman was almost overpowering.

'Aunty Lou,' whispered Biddy. 'She's leaving things everywhere.' She led Angela on tiptoe to a drawer in the cubist room-divider. There was no smell there; only a wrinkled, dirty knitting pattern for a scarf, dated 1954; little ends of grey and maroon wool, and endless wrappers from Mentholyptus sweets, tightly screwed up. 'I've been finding them for a week; I get up first in the morning, to get to them before Roger does. If he knew, he'd go crazy.'

'But someone's *leaving* them there,' shouted Angela. 'Someone's leaving them around deliberately.'

'Who do we know that sucks Mentholyptus sweets, or knits?' said Biddy hopelessly, and began to cry.

When Angela had finally calmed her down, she gathered all

the evidence up into her handbag and went back home to Peter, with a look on her face that had never been there before. She burst into the Haunted Mansion like the wrath of God. Straight to his study. He had been working; there was a half-finished page in the typewriter, a smouldering fag-end in the full ashtray and a number of fresh breadcrumbs on the floor. But he wasn't there. She searched the house; nothing. Went back to his study, anxious now as well as angry. She looked out of the window, and nearly screamed.

He was only two yards away, outside the window. But so still, she hadn't noticed him. He was standing studying a rose tree, the one with red roses that he alleged had once telepathed to him. Telepathed 'I love you'. But he wasn't telepathing this morning; he was watching the slow progress of a small green caterpillar up a leaf, with a look of infinite affection on his face. The white cat was crouched, equally attentive, on his shoulder. It was clear what *she* would like to do to the caterpillar, but Peter had a gently restraining hand on her back. He often stood like this for ten minutes on end; as if time didn't matter. The first time she had caught him like that was the moment she fell in love with him. But she didn't feel the least in love with him now. She stormed up to him and opened her handbag. His eyes swam up to her, as out of a faraway dream. He smiled, and said:

'You *have* had a good morning's shopping. That knitting must have been a real bargain—'

'Don't you treat me like a child!' she shouted. 'And don't you lie to me!'

He looked gently hurt; she'd never had cause to shout at him before.

'What am I supposed to have done?'

'You know damn well what you've done. Poking these things down the back of Biddy's furniture, dropping them under the settee every time we go. And writing those revolting cards. And that stupid business at Blackpool . . . You've got Biddy frightened out of her wits, and Roger.'

'I'm sorry about Biddy,' he said slowly. And meant it. 'But as for Roger—'

'What has Roger ever done to you?'

'Tried to get me into shape,' said Peter, pulling a fold of flesh out from his paunch. 'And getting me called "Hairy Ape" from the first day I went to Flamborough Grammar. And keeping me off the cricket team for a year, after he was made captain. And trying to scare me that his rotten little adding-machines are going to take over the world. Will that do?'

'Don't be so bloody childish!' she shouted. Then she saw the look in his eyes, and had to steel herself to say:

'Either you go and tell them the truth. Or I will.'

'Thank you for your loyalty . . .'

'Well, at least I came back and told you. If you *don't* tell them, I'm not sure I shall have anything I want to be loyal to.'

That brought him up sharply. He thought for a moment, then shrugged.

'It was only a joke.'

'Well, the joke's over now. We'll go and tell Biddy straight away.'

'We will go and tell Biddy tomorrow; I have work to do today.'

'Like watching bloody caterpillars.'

'Like watching bloody caterpillars.' She knew there would be no further moving him; and she suddenly found all her courage gone. She went and made a very light lunch, which they ate in mutual bad-temper and silence. After he had eaten his share, Peter went and ostentatiously helped himself to several more chunks from the bread bin.

Next morning, bright and early, they drove round to Mission

Control together. Roger's new Daimler was still on the drive, though he was normally away to work by eight. Some of the curtains were still drawn; the others were pulled back wildly. The milk was still outside the door. Somehow, it made Angela irrationally afraid, so she pushed the bell-push longer and harder than usual, to drive her fear out.

Biddy answered the door in a house-coat, her hair screwed back in an elastic band. She wore no make-up, and she looked dreadful. She led them into the big through-lounge. The half-open curtains made a harsh diagonal streak of bright sunlight across the floor, leaving the rest of the room dramatically dark. Roger was sitting with a coffee mug in his hand, without shoes or tie. His usually-immaculate shirt and trousers looked as if they'd been slept in. They sat down awkwardly, as if this were a house of bereavement. Roger silently held a card out to Angela. It was a view of Flamborough; the half-timbered Moot Hall. On the back, in the same awful writing, it was addressed to Mrs Louise Brown. At the address of Mission Control itself. It said:

Dear Aunty Lou, Hope you are getting nicely settled in for your little stay with our Roger and his lady-wife. We will be looking in in a day or two, to see how you are getting on.
All the best,
Fred and Alice

Angela looked up at Biddy and Roger, as they sat side by side opposite her. She smiled.

'Don't worry. We can explain everything.'

'Can you?' said Roger listlessly.

Angela looked nervously at Peter. He gave a quick nod of permission, from where he was hunched darkly in an armchair.

'It was all a practical joke,' said Angela, with a failed laugh that didn't lift the atmosphere an inch. 'Peter thought it up to – to amuse you. The cards, the sweet-wrappers, the knitting. Everything. It was just Peter, having a . . . lark.'

Roger turned to look at Peter; it was impossible to see either of their faces, in the semi-dark.

'Thanks, mate,' said Roger, with a savagery that took Angela's breath away.

'Can't you even take a little joke?' relied Peter, with equal savagery. 'Anyway, it's all over now.'

'Is it?' shouted Roger. '*Is* it? Haven't you got a sense of *smell* either?'

And Angela suddenly realized the other thing that was making the room so dreadful. The sweet smell of sick old age filled it; the smell of dirty underwear and bedpans, camphor and aniseed, and hopelessness. It took her back nearly all her twenty-four years to when Grandad had died.

'How are you managing this effect, clever-dick?' shouted Roger. 'Throwing crap around by the bucketful? Look!' He pointed to the rows of air-fresheners and aerosols that stood on every shelf; they heard the extractor fans roaring in the kitchen and bathroom, sounding as loud, suddenly, as aero-engines.

For the first time, Peter looked genuinely put-out. 'Sure it's not the drains?' he asked, feebly.

'There's not a trace of this smell upstairs,' said Biddy tightly. 'Nor in the garage or the utility-room. It's all in here. She's only in here.'

'How did you know about her?' shouted Roger, straight through Biddy's voice. 'How did you know she *existed*?'

'Who?' asked Peter, stupidly.

'Aunty Lou,' said Roger. 'Oh yes. You see, there really was an Aunty Lou. There really was a Fred and Alice. I lived with them for three months, when I was five. My parents had to go abroad and left me with my grandmother. But my grandmother got ill and had to go into hospital, and I was left in the charge of her cook and gardener, Alice and Fred. And the moment she'd gone into hospital, they imported this ghastly Lou creature, into my grandmother's bedroom. And there she stayed, till my grandmother got better. And I had to fetch and carry for her – she was bedridden – and the morning before my grandmother came back, she grabbed me by my arm and made me give her a kiss. Then she made me promise to come back and see her, when I was a famous man. She said, "You won't forget your old Aunty Lou, will you, dear?" And she pinched my cheek. God, I've never loathed anybody so much in my life. But I never told anybody about her. Nobody in Flamborough. I'd have died rather than tell anybody. *So how did you know?*' He leaned across and grabbed Peter by his coat.

They all looked at Peter.

'I didn't,' said Peter. 'I just made the names up, when we were sitting round the dining table that night. The names just came into my head . . . they were the vulgarest names I could think of. A little newsagent I know wrote the cards for me. William Short in the Bullring, ask him.'

'I never saw *their* writing,' said Roger. Then, suddenly, alarmingly at a tangent, he shouted, 'Can't you hear anything?'

There was a silence, while they all listened.

'Two extractor fans,' said Peter, with false flippancy. He was never normally flippant. Angela could tell how shaken he was, and it frightened her. Suddenly the thing was no longer funny old eccentric Peter. Biddy walked out stiffly and switched off the fans. They listened again. Angela said:

'Will you all stop breathing a minute. Please!' She listened till her lungs threatened to burst, then let her breath out in a great rush, gasped, choked, and then said, 'I thought I could hear somebody breathing.'

'Yes,' said Roger bitterly. 'Somebody breathing. Somebody with a bad chest – somebody with asthma.'

'Ye . . . es,' said Angela.

'And nobody here's got asthma – not even our nicotine-stained friend there, though he deserves to have. Well, Aunty Lou had asthma. And how.'

Biddy gave a shudder, and clutched her arms across her bosom. They were all four silent again, listening to the noise of the asthmatic breathing. Or was it? Angela's mind rebelled. Surely it was traffic on the main road, or some monotonous industrial plant, far away. Or the swish of blood in her own ears. It was so much everywhere, so soft and so regular, you couldn't tell. The human mind is infinitely suggestible, she told herself.

But she had mentioned 'breathing' before anyone had said a word . . .

After a while, Roger began to speak in a curiously flat voice. As if everything that was happening at this moment had happened long ago in the past.

'The card came yesterday lunchtime, after you'd gone, Angela. By the time I got home, Biddy was in quite a state, going on about sweet papers. Then she told me you'd taken all the evidence and, well, we're not fools . . . I think I relaxed for the first time in days. Had a few whiskies, watched the telly and planned just exactly what I would do to his lordship there when I finally caught up with him.

'I must have dozed off – slept, in fact, slept quite a long time. I must have half come round about midnight, because the weather-man was mouthing on over his troughs of low pressure, and the fire was very low, and it was bloody cold. I remember thinking that Biddy must have turned the central-heating thermostat down, and I think I called out to her to go and turn it up, but I didn't get any reply; and I sort of dozed off again. Then I heard somebody moving very softly round the room, and I thought it was Biddy seeing to things for the morning and not wanting to wake me. I think I said something to her, but again she didn't reply. But the moving about went on. Then I thought, she's moving very oddly, like an old woman, like an invalid. Has she hurt herself? And then I smelt that smell, really strongly for the first time, and I knew who it reminded me of – I'd been trying to remember for days, only the smell was fainter then – and I must have had a dream because I was back in Grandmother's house with that . . . thing, and it was saying to me, "You will come back and see me when you're rich and famous."

'And I felt a hand on my cheek.

'Then I woke up, and the room was icy and my legs were all pins-and-needles so I could hardly walk. I was reeling about calling, "Biddy, Biddy, I've had such a horrible dream." But she was nowhere about. I staggered to the bedroom, and there was Biddy, snoring – obviously been snoring for hours. I couldn't even waken her.'

'The doctor's given me some pills,' said Biddy. 'They knock me out like a light. I'd gone to bed and left Roger at ten, I felt so tired.'

There was another silence.

'I'm sorry,' said Peter. 'I'll not say I didn't mean to upset you; but nothing like this.'

'Oh, don't worry,' said Roger savagely. 'You might have thought you were using them, but actually, *they* were using *you*. To get hold of me again. You must be a sort of medium, or something.'

'There's a bit of it in our family – my mother's got a bit. But–' and he looked round as if he was speaking at the walls– '*I* don't like being used.' He wandered off, touring the house. They could hear him saying, from time to time:

'*I* don't like being *used*.'

Angela grinned at Roger and Biddy in weak apology. They

grinned back at her, in weak apology. Biddy got up and pulled back the curtains fully. Light flooded into the room, and they shook themselves like dogs shaking off water after a swim.

'Maybe if you got away for a few days . . .' said Angela.

Roger shook his head. 'Have you smelt inside my Daimler?' he asked. 'Have you smelt inside Biddy's Mini?'

They drove back home.

'Well, what do you make of it?' asked Angela.

'I don't like being *used*,' said Peter. He sounded more angry than he had been with Roger in the beginning.

'But surely there's some explanation . . . is it Roger's mind, taking over where you left off? Did you upset him and . . . the human mind's a funny thing.'

'Who do you think he is?' said Peter, rudely. 'Uri Geller? I've never smelt a smell like that in all my life.'

'Don't be so cross.'

'I don't like being *used*,' Peter repeated. And he stalked off to his study, where he sat for about five hours, with the brindle cat on his knee and the white cat draped luxuriously over his shoulder.

Angela, feeling she must do something, went to see William Short, Peter's 'little newsagent'. He was a ginger-moustached man, self-important but eager to please Mr Wingfield's wife. Yes, he had written the Christmas card for Mr Wingfield. Yes, he had gone on the pensioners' outing to Blackpool, with his missus and her mother. Yes, they had forged false names. But they'd had a lovely time, thanks to Mr Wingfield. All that expense, too, just for a joke. Mr Wingfield mustn't be short of a penny.

He dutifully wrote her some words on a postcard, plucked from a bundle in his fly-blown window. *My constant desire is to give the best possible service to all my customers at all times, signed, best regards, William Short.*

Angela took the Blackpool card from her handbag, and compared them. The handwriting was similar, typical, elderly, working-class writing. But it was not the same.

'That's not my writing,' said William Short. 'It's my biro and it's the card I used, but it's not my writing. Hey, what's the game?' He took a lot of getting rid of; especially as Angela herself was on the verge of hysterics.

As she opened the front door of the Haunted Mansion, the phone was ringing. Ringing in a violent way in a darkened house; ringing in a way that could only mean bad trouble. Angela picked it up, trembling.

It was Biddy, calling from a hospital in Birmingham. Crying so much she could hardly speak. Finally, she got it out. Roger had determined to carry on with his day, in spite of everything. He had driven up to Birmingham for an afternoon conference; gone mad on the M1, driven across the central reservation at eighty miles an hour, been slowed by the central barrier, but finally rolled over it into the path . . . It had been, again, a miracle he had got out alive. He had a fractured pelvis and two broken legs, and had been in the operating theatre three hours. The surgeons had been sure they had saved his life, but his whole system was not responding.

'He's giving up,' said Biddy, dully. 'And the room he's in is full of that smell. The surgeon gave the intensive-care sister a rocket about it, and she's going frantic . . .'

There was nothing Angela could find to say, till Biddy rang off. Then she looked up and gave a little scream. Peter had come up to her softly in the dark.

'I heard,' he said. 'I heard it all on the extension.'

'We must *do* something.'

'It's too late.'

Something in his voice made her say, 'Too late for what, Peter?'

'Nothing.'

But somehow she knew. 'I'm going round to Mission Control,' she said.

'What the hell for?' There was panic in his voice. She groped round desperately for an excuse.

'Biddy asked me to feed her budgie.'

'Biddy hasn't got a budgie. Roger won't have a pet in the house.'

'It's in her sewing-room. He lets her do what she likes in there.'

He reached to stop her going, but she had fled out through the still-open door and was running to her car. Luckily the keys were still in her hand. She swung out of the drive with the driver's door ajar.

She didn't drive fast; Peter would have to get the garage open, and get his own car out. And she didn't want to arrive at Mission Control one second before he did.

She saw his yellow Volkswagen Beetle turn into the road as she turned into Biddy's drive. She had just time to lift up the plant pot in the garage, where Biddy – without Roger's knowledge – always left a key. As she walked up to the front door, Peter screeched to a stop behind her, throwing up gravel clumsily in all directions.

She put the key in the lock, and hesitated. There was a flickering blue light from Biddy's lounge. The flicker of a *black-and-white* television. And there was the sound of raucous studio laughter. A stupid, brainless, hateful programme, the kind that nobody who knew Roger and Biddy would ever watch.

She heard Peter's step just behind her, and swung open the front door and ran for the lounge, knocking her thighs painfully into things as she ran. She opened the door. The smell was overpowering, choking. And they were there, sitting, turning their faces in the blue flicker, out of the dark, to look at her.

Fred, Alice and Aunty Lou. They were exactly as Peter had described them. Of course. And she noticed that where they sat, the cushions were deeply dented. They said nothing, just stared at her; Alice's spectacles reflected the shape of the telly, a glowing white rectangle, so that she seemed to have goat's eyes. Aunty Lou had a shawl round her head, so you couldn't see her face at all. There was a little table beside her, laden with medicine bottles.

Fred gestured for Angela to sit down, and she found she could not refuse. She sat down on the settee next to him; felt his weight respond on the other end of it as she sat. Felt the cold radiating out of his body. On the floor all round his slippers, and on the cushions of the couch, she could see little crumbly crumbs of black stuff. The sharp smell of earth came to her, through the smell of Aunty Lou.

She had to touch him; she didn't want to, and yet she had to. She had to *know*. She reached out a trembling finger, and poked as in a dream.

He was solid, damp and icy cold. She wanted to scream, but couldn't; the scream filled her head till she thought her head was going to burst.

Peter came in. Then she knew why he had taken so long. He was carrying the white cat in his arms, and the little brindled cat sat on his shoulder. They both looked electrified, backs plumed and tails bushed, so they looked twice their normal size. Their huge eyes, like black marbles, never left Fred, Alice and Aunty Lou. Angela sensed, dimly, that the struggle had already begun.

Peter walked across to the set; it was the twenty-four-inch colour set that Roger had always had; but, in a black-and-white flicker, something called *The Army Game* was just ending. Peter turned a switch and stared rudely at Fred, his beard stuck out, which was Peter at his most aggressive. Immediately, the black-and-white image on the screen flickered and faded, then regained strength. Then faded again.

Then the real colour came on – Robin Day, mouthing silently. Then black-and-white, colour, black-and-white, colour. In some ways, the colour was worse, for its brighter reflected light showed up the colours that Fred, Alice and Aunty Lou really were. Which did not bear thinking about. And the mounds of black soil round their feet . . .

Finally, Robin Day was established; his voice came through loud and clear, giving stick to some shadow-cabinet minister. Angela closed her eyes, and for the first and last time in her life, sought refuge in the bosom of Robin Day. But she could still feel the conflicts raging round her; the laden cold clouds that were Fred, Alice and Aunty Lou; the burning, growing, slow anger that was Peter, and the lightning-stabbing eyes of the two cats.

To think, thought Angela, far away, that those two cats have slept all night on my bed . . .

Someone was splashing water on her face.

Why was Peter splashing water on her face? Come to that, why was she lying on the floor? Was it one of Roger's rather superior, spiteful party games?

Then she remembered Roger was in Birmingham, dying. It all came back to her in a terrible flood. She sat up, making her head spin, and stared round wildly.

The lounge was fully-lit; every movable spotlight in the place was on. The telly was off, and the whole place looked quite normal; immaculate, except for the drying crumbs of soil on the carpet and couch where— The two cats were sniffing them, then scratching round them, as if trying to bury them. A lot of nylon carpet-tufts were flying; the sound of ripping claws was horrendous.

Immediately a door slammed in her mind. Fred, Alice, and Aunty Lou had never existed. Not here, in this tidy, rational, luxurious room . . . Then the door in her mind began to drift open again: memories of the *feel* of them.

'It's all right, they've gone,' said Peter. He looked pale and there were beads of sweat on his upper lip.

'For *good*?'

'As far as *we're* concerned.'

'What happened?'

'We were losing, especially after you conked out – you were helping, you know, just by being here. If it hadn't been for the cats, they'd have had me, for sure – you'd have wakened up to find me dead, probably, and them still there, grinning at you as you came round.'

Her very mind retched.

'All *right*,' said Peter. 'You're all right now. I knew it would be rough; why d'you think you had to force me to come? God, I never want to go through anything like *that* again. Anyway, I knew they'd used some part of my mind, to manifest themselves in the first place. If only I could find that part of me, and cut the wire, so to speak, we'd be OK. Like opening and defusing a bomb. But which part of my mind? I just couldn't seem to find it, and they were getting colder and heavier on me all the time. I remember thinking, *Poor* old Rog has had it . . . and then the three of them just went pop like balloons.'

'Compassion,' said Angela. 'You were sorry for Rog, you didn't hate him any more; they were using your hate.'

'Shan't hate him again in a hurry,' said Peter. 'For my sake.'

Out in the hall, the phone was ringing. 'I'll get it,' said Angela, scrambling to her feet.

'Thanks,' said Peter, and sat down heavily among the crumbs of soil.

It was Biddy on the phone, ringing from Birmingham, gabbling with relief. 'He's rallied. They say he's rallied. They say he's going to make it.'

'Thank God,' said Angela, and many other soft, soothing, thankful, meaningless phrases, until Biddy said she must go back to the ward. Then a thought occurred to Angela. 'How did you know we'd be here?'

'Well,' said Biddy, 'I tried to ring you at home . . . and the smell suddenly went, when Roger started to rally. I knew Peter had managed it somehow. Isn't he *wonderful*?'

'Hmmmmm,' said Angela. She was by nature tactful.

As she put down the phone, she suddenly realized that the whole house reeked of pine air freshener.

St Austin Friars

The church of St Austin Friars stands in an inner suburb of Muncaster. It is huge for a parish church, beautiful in the Perpendicular style, and black as coal from the smoke of the city. It stands on a hill, amidst its long-disused graveyard, and its only near companion is the Greek Revival rectory, like a temple with chimneys, also coal-black. It is really St Margaret's, but Muncastrians always call it St Austin Friars, in memory of the Augustinian canons who had their monastery there in the Middle Ages.

Then, it stood in fair countryside, amidst its own rich demesne. Muncaster was no more than the houses of the monastic servants. But the Industrial Revolution came to Muncaster and it grew, covering all the green fields and hills with soot and sweat and money. By the time that the Reverend Martin Williams was appointed rector in 1970, the only traces of the monastery, apart from the church, were a mean street called Fishponds and another called Cloister Lane.

Martin Williams came when the Industrial Revolution was departing, having had its way with Muncaster. The day after he moved into the rectory, the houses of Fishponds were being demolished. The dust from falling brick and the smoke from the scrap-wood fires were so engulfing that the demolition foreman, a decent man, came up to the rectory to apologize.

'You'll soon be shot of us,' he said, sitting down to a mug of tea that Sheila, as a well-trained clergy wife, immediately laid before him. 'Trouble is, you'll soon be shot o' your parish, too. It's all going, you know!'

'Yes, I know,' said Martin, sticking his hands into the pockets of long thin trousers, and staring out of the window. 'It's a shame.'

'Shame nothing!' said the foreman. 'Seen a mort o' suffering, this place. Bringing up fo'teen bairns on a pound a week in a room no bigger nor your pantry. Beggin' yer pardon, missus. But me dad an' me grandad told me about it. Had an evil name, round here. Cholera – typhoid – afore they got the drains right. Four hundred dead in one week, they say; one long hot summer. Good riddance to bad rubbish, *I* say.'

'Aren't they going to build multi-storey flats instead?' asked Sheila.

'Not that *I* heard,' said the foreman. 'Not that they tell the likes of us anything. Other parts, people are crying their hearts out 'cause they're having to leave, but not in Fishponds. They can't wait to get out to the overspill. What you aiming to do wi' yersel, then?'

Martin gave a violent start; he still could not get used to the sudden bluntness of the North, after his last curacy in Kent. Here, people asked you the most intimate questions the moment they'd shaken hands. This chap would be asking next when they were going to start a family.

'What am I going to do with myself? Well, it just so happens that the city centre is also part of this parish. So I'll be down there a lot . . .'

'*They're* a right queer push an' all,' opined the foreman, drinking deep into his mug and, to Sheila's fascination, actually wiping his moustache with the back of his hand. 'Pimps, prostitutes, homosexuals, actors – what's the difference? Beggin' yer pardon, missus.'

'Jesus mixed with prostitutes and sinners,' said Martin,

giving him a look of sharp blue charity that had the foreman on his feet in a second.

'Thank you for the tea, missus. And—' he gave Martin a sharp look in return— 'best o' luck wi' the city centre. Yer might just do something down *there* – wi' luck. All the best.' And he wiped his hands on the seat of his trousers, shook both their hands, and departed. His boots, crunching down the long drive, left that peculiar silence that lay like the black dust all over the rectory, and that Martin and Sheila were to come to know so well.

'I don't like this place,' said Sheila, washing up the mug to break the silence.

'I know you don't,' said Martin. 'But it's a good living, and a good city – think of all the concerts we can go to. And you'll be out teaching most of the time. And out in the evenings. We'll hardly be in the place – just camping out.'

The kitchen was large and fully-fitted. Equipped down to a Kenwood mixer, and not a thing in it was theirs. Pity the main areas of formica were in a spirit-lowering shade of browny-purple . . .

All the many rooms were the same: beautifully decorated, beautifully furnished. The sitting-room had leather settees and couches, hardly touched. The whole house was recently wired, totally weatherproof and structurally immaculate. There wasn't a bit of do-it-yourself for Martin or Sheila to lay their fingers on.

'Canon Maitland must have been awfully well-off, to afford all this,' said Sheila. 'And no one to leave it all to when he died.'

'He was *very* old,' said Martin. 'Ninety-four.'

'But they're supposed to retire at seventy.'

'This place was special. Very little work, even before the demolition. The Bishop told me.' The Bishop had told him many things.

The Bishop was an old-school-tie friend of Martin's previous bishop in Kent. The Bishop had wanted a bright young man, willing to try unorthodox methods in a city-centre parish. And to be one of the Bishop's chaplains, which mainly involved marking high-level clergy exam-papers. And to be a one-day-a-week lecturer in Christian Social Work at the Church of England college. 'Plenty of interesting things to fill your week, young man. Don't you worry your head about Fishponds and Cloister Lane,' the Bishop had said, hand on Martin's shoulder, when Martin finally accepted the job, without consulting Sheila first (a sore point).

But in spite of this, for a year they were happy. Sheila enjoyed her school, and Martin his college. Three days a week he worked his city-centre parish, using the back rooms of ornate Edwardian pubs such as The Grapes, drinking half-pints of shandy carefully, and eating a lot of curious pub-grub. He knew enough to wear a sports-coat and cover his clergyman's dog collar with a polo-neck sweater (except when a clergyman was actually required, when he would roll down the neck of the sweater to reveal all). By the time the pimps and prostitutes, actors and homosexuals found out he was a clergyman, they'd also found out that he was a good sort, a good listener, a good shoulder to cry on, and good for a bed for the night in a crisis. He was *quite* wise, but he was *very* nice; he helped a number of people to avoid committing suicide, simply because, in the moment of the act, they thought how upset he would be, how disappointed if they really did it. A lot of the men kept his card and phone number in their jacket; a lot of the girls brought him home-knitted sweaters and jars of jam their mums had made. A certain number of girls tried to persuade him into bed with them, in the cause of the New Theology, but he always got away by saying, 'Not while on duty.' He was always on duty. Sheila stored the pullovers (most of which didn't fit, but none of which he would throw away) in a large cupboard, and lined the shelves of the pantry with the jars of jam. They weren't for eating, Martin said, they were for looking at. Sheila was pretty philosophical; anybody who married Martin would have had to be philosophical.

They went to lots of concerts; threw lots of parties, full of drunken radical social workers, militant black leaders, manic-depressive pimps and nymphomaniac Liberal debutantes. The isolated rectory kept their secret; there was no complaint to the Bishop. But when the last of the guests had gone, the rectory returned to its own secrets.

Meanwhile, the demolition continued. Cloister Lane went, and Infirmary Street, and Boundary Road. Every time Martin looked out of the window, the battered gable-ends of the houses, defiantly flaunting their tattered wallpaper through wind and rain, seemed to get further away. Martin got the strange idea that the whole city was recoiling from St Austin Friars, like the crowd at a circus when the tiger gets loose. He told himself not to be silly. Sheila told him not to be silly. They were living in clover.

The congregation at Sunday service was three: Sheila, and the two church-wardens. One warden, Mr Phillips, was also verger and caretaker. The other, Mr Rubens, was said to be the city's last big pawnbroker. Dark, solid, formal and sleek, he wasn't the kind of man you could ask that kind of question. The congregation on Wednesday morning was nil; Martin said the service alone in the great, dark, hollow church. He would have liked to sing it, but there were too many echoes answering, and he soon gave it up. He recognized this as his first defeat.

It was all defeats, as far as the church services were concerned. He went round the poor houses and corner shops that were left, beyond Fishponds and Cloister Lane. The people were respectful, sickeningly respectful. He tried to be friendly, but they treated him as if he were a pope, and not a jolly pope, either. If there was a crowd in a shop, they stood aside deferentially to let him buy his cigarettes, then listened silently, hushed, to his remarks about the weather or the football team. Waiting for him to go, so they could resume their whispering, scurrying, mouse-like lives. If he called at a house, he was sat in the tiny, freezing front parlour, while the housewife sent out for expensive cakes and the children peeped round the door at him, and fled when he spoke to them. They gave him horrifying amounts of money, 'for the church'. One pensioner gave him a five pound note, though her stockings were darned and her shoes cracked. When he tried to refuse it, she burst into tears, pleading with him to take it, and would not be pacified until he did. He thought, bitterly, that they never saw *him* at all; they saw another Canon Maitland, or some other Victorian tyrant-priest. He was walking in another man's shoes. He hated that man; he would have strangled that man if he could. But that man was invisible; close to him as his own skin. None of the local people came to church; they were paying him to go away and leave them in peace.

He had better luck with his city-centre people; sometimes they came to church for love of him: a group of actors from the Library Theatre, theatrically muffled in long scarves and wide-brimmed black hats; once, a bunch of the girls, in fun-furs, mini-skirts and suede boots. They hadn't a clue how to take part in the service, and they caused an explosion at the churchwardens' meeting afterwards. Mr Phillips, whose house now stood out of the flat, spreading clearances like a decaying Gothic tooth, said that the likes of them were not fit to be seen in church. His bitten grey moustache and his pendulous jowls wobbled in hideous indignation. But the smooth Mr Rubens cut him short.

'Father Williams is entitled to have anyone he likes in his

church. Your job is to keep it clean and ring the bell.' Mr Phillips came to heel like a whipped cur; which taught Martin a lot. Mr Rubens cracked the whip. Mr Rubens got things done.

Like the strange matter of the choir. Martin had discovered a moth-balled oak wardrobe, full of red and white choir vestments. He said wistfully at one meeting that he *would* like to have a choir. The next Sunday, he was amazed to find he had a choir, of total strangers, complete with organist and choirmaster. They sang beautifully. But in conversation with one child in the vestry afterwards, he found they were a school choir, bussed in from a distance at considerable expense, and quite obviously doing it for the money. When he pointed out to Mr Rubens that this was not what he had meant at all, Mr Rubens looked at him very sharply and said he wouldn't be bothered with them again. Just as long as he made up his mind what he wanted. Martin began to feel like somebody's pampered mistress. But he was growing a little afraid of Mr Rubens. For one thing, Mr Rubens had never given his address or phone number. He always rang Martin; he was the one that fixed the churchwardens' meetings.

Afterwards, Martin realized he should have got out of St Austin's then. But the Bishop was pleased with all the work he was doing; and Mr Rubens had told the Bishop that he was *delighted* with all the work Martin was doing. And everything but St Austin's was going so well.

St Austin's got worse and worse. Martin loved churches, but he couldn't love St Austin's. It wasn't spooky exactly, just infinitely old and cold and dark. It rejected him. He had the vestry redecorated in contemporary style, installed a vinyl-topped desk and telephone, hung framed prints of the Turin Shroud and Dali's modern Crucifixion on the wall. He would make that, at least, a place where people came, for coffee and a chat when they had a problem. Nobody came.

Still, Martin bravely persisted in his church, like an occupying army, for three hours every Wednesday morning. After the service, he drifted up the aisles reading the epitaphs of long-dead Muncastrians, engraved on Georgian and Regency marble on the walls.

Near this spot are buried the Mortal Remains of Jonathan Appleby Esq, who died on the 14th of February, 1828, aetat 17 yeers.

For those who never knew him, no words can convey his Infinite Excellence of Character.

As for his grieving Friends, who had the Infinite Privilege of his Acquaintanceship, they are silenced by Greefe.

Therefore, no word Further is Uttered.

Tactful, that, thought Martin with a wry grin. But grave humour is thin gruel to the human heart, and on the whole the epitaphs did not console him. He did, however, notice a preponderance of odd names. *Canzo. Frederick Canzo, William Ewart Canzo, Joshua Canzo.* And *Betyl.* And *Morsk.* But especially the name *Drogo* cropped up. There must be more Drogos buried in the crypt under the church than all the rest put together. Funny, how these odd names had died out. He had never met a Canzo or a Betyl or a Morsk or a Drogo in his life.

One Wednesday morning he was amazed to hear the phone ringing, at the far end of the church. He ran so eagerly, he arrived quite out of breath. The only person who had ever rung him until now was Sheila from the rectory, to tell him lunch was ready. But at this moment she would be hard at it, teaching.

'St Margaret's church. Can I help you?'

'That St Austin Friars?'

'Yes.'

'Why didn't you say so? We've got a funeral for you.'

'Wait, let me find the diary and a pencil. Now where did I – ah good. Right.' Martin was practically gabbling, at the idea of actually being useful for a change. 'Who's speaking?'

'This is Bettle's, the undertakers. Deceased's name is William Henry Drogo. Yes, that's right, D-R-O-G-O. Friday morning, 28th March at 10.30 a.m.'

Martin glanced over his shoulder at the Mowbray's calendar on the wall. Today was Wednesday the 26th. 'Fine,' he said. 'Will you want the bell rung?'

'Old Phillips knows how we like it. Leave it to him.'

'And your telephone number?'

'Muncaster 213245.' The voice sounded grudging. 'Phillips will fill you in.' There was a click and the speaker was gone.

Martin looked down at the details in his diary. Strange, the name Drogo cropping up, just when he'd been telling himself that such names must be dead and gone. Usual kind of service, he supposed. No request for a special sermon.

It was then that he realized that today was not Wednesday the 26th of March.

It was only Wednesday the 26th of February. Somebody had booked a funeral a month in advance.

Martin rang the number back.

'Excuse me, I think you've made some mistake. I think you want Mr Drogo buried on the 28th February. You said the 28th of March. It's a mistake that's easily made – I often make it—'

'When I say the 28th of March,' said the voice, very Muncastrian, 'I *mean* the 28th of March.'

'But—'

'Ask old Phillips.' The phone went down with an extra-loud click, and when Martin re-dialled, the other end didn't answer.

At first, he was sure it was a practical joker. Especially as he went through the telephone directory and could find no undertaker called Bettle. Or Beddle. Or Bethel, for that matter. Nor Bettell, nor Bettall. So then he looked up Drogo.

To his surprise, there were quite a lot of Drogos – eight in all, including *Drogo's, Pharmaceutical Suppliers and Whole-salers*. And a *Drogo, William H.*, at a very lush address in Willington, out in the fresh air in the foothills of the Pennines.

Martin paced up and down the vestry in a rare taking. Of course, he could always ask old Phillips, as he'd been told. But he had a certain reluctance to be laughed at by old Phillips. There must be other ways to check . . .

William H. Drogo was a man of importance – perhaps the chairman of Drogo Pharmaceuticals? Heart pounding, he rang Drogo Pharmaceuticals and asked for William H. Drogo. Yes, a very expensive female voice answered, Mr William H. Drogo was chairman. Yes, Mr William *Henry* Drogo. But unfortunately he was not available, being out all day at a meeting in London. If Mr . . .? – Mr Williams would care to ring back tomorrow . . .?

'Are there any other William Henry Drogos?'

No. The expensive voice allowed itself to sound faintly offended. There was only one Mr William Henry Drogo. And she knew the *whole* family. There *was* only one Drogo family, at least in Britain. The voice curved upwards, making the Drogos sound more distinctive than the Royal Family.

Martin rang off, before he was reduced to sounding a complete blithering idiot.

He took to pacing up and down again. That expensive voice . . . that imperturbable voice . . . would be quite calm enough to effect a cover-up. Why a cover-up? Perhaps for commercial reasons. Some firms were pretty vulnerable when the big boss-man suddenly died. But you couldn't cover up a death for a month, for God's sake . . . Feeling even more of an idiot, but rather cross just the same, he rang the Drogo home number. This time a deep female voice answered; a voice so rich and exotic, it made the other female voice sound plastic.

'I'm sorry, Mr . . . Williams. My grandfather is away in London all day today. If you rang his office in the morning, I'm sure he'd be delighted to speak to you.'

He hung up. That was certainly no house of mourning, no house shaken to the roots by a death. That house was smug, rich, utterly certain of itself, full of the careless decency that comes from years without pain. It was a hoax. He wouldn't ask old Phillips. It was probably old Phillips who had made the hoax call. Who else knew all about the Drogos lining the aisles of his church with their memorials? Drogos and Canzos and Morsks and Betyls.

Betyl. Not Bettle the undertaker, but Betyl the undertaker.

Oh, don't be crazy. Whoever heard of anyone called Betyl?

Whoever had heard of anyone called Drogo? He reached for the telephone directory.

No *Betyl.*

Then he realized that the current directory was held up by a pile of other directors, well-nibbled by the church mice and rather damp towards the bottom of the heap.

In the rotting, falling-apart 1953 directory, he found it. *Betyl Georg & Son, Funeral Directors, 4 Albert St, Hathershaw. Muncaster 213245.* Hathershaw was the next inner suburb, only two miles away.

Feeling slightly unreal, he got out the car and drove over.

Hathershaw was in the throes of demolition, too. It was like fleeing through a doomed city. Houses first slateless, then roofless, then windowless. Streets that were only pavements and cobbles and solitary lampposts on corners; streets pressed flat like wild flowers in a book. Streets with no names, just old Victorian manhole-covers. Fires on every mound of fallen brick. Bulldozers; sweating, filthy, rejoicing demolition men.

'Albert Street?' yelled Martin, winding down his window and trying to compete against another wall falling down.

'You'll be lucky, squire. If you're quick, you might just catch it before it goes. Third right, second left. Mind yer head.'

He caught it. The slates were just coming off the roof of Number 4. The bulldozers were three houses away.

Georg Betyl and Son. Funeral Directors. Established 1832.

The shop window was still draped in faded ecclesiastical purple. There were three black urns, tastelessly arranged, and a squat marble box for flowers, labelled *From friends and neighbours.*

'Stop!' shouted Martin, leaping from his car. The demolition team was facetious, but not unsympathetic.

'Yeah,' said the gaffer, to his request for admittance. 'Why not? It won't be here by five o'clock.' They smashed in the black, rather nice Georgian front door with a sledge-hammer, while Martin winced.

Inside, the place felt odd already, with half the roof stripped. There was the phone; dead when Martin picked it up.

'GPO was here an hour ago, to cut it off,' said the gaffer. 'If you want that phone, you can have it,' he added generously. 'Cost you a quid – you don't get many like that, these days.' There was also an ancient iron safe, door hanging open, some cremation urns in white plastic, and a tin waste-bucket full of empty envelopes addressed to *Georg Betyl and Son, Funeral Directors, 4 Albert Street, Hathershaw* and going back sixty years. Two old wooden chairs, and nothing else at all.

*

The next day, Martin rang GPO telephones. They were unable to help; all communications and bills for Mr Betyl had always been sent to 4 Albert Street. As far as they were concerned, Mr Betyl had paid his terminal bill and ceased to exist. There had certainly been no application for a new telephone number at a new address. Muncaster Corporation also did their best; yes, they had purchased the shop from Mr Betyl; and had sent all correspondence and the final purchase cheque to 4 Albert Street. No, he was only on their rolls of electors at the Albert Street address. Perhaps he had lived above the shop?

Feeling the boldness of despair, Martin rang Drogo Pharmaceuticals again. The expensive voice (who knew something more about him than she had known the previous day) put him straight through to Mr William Henry Drogo.

'I don't know how to start,' said Martin, suddenly helpless.

'You sound rather upset.' Drogo's voice had the same richness as his granddaughter's.

'I am a little upset. There's something I have to tell you.'

'You are the new rector of St Austin Friars.'

'Yes. How did you know that?'

'I've always had an interest in St Austin's,' said Mr Drogo. 'Perhaps you would honour my granddaughter and me with your company at dinner tomorrow night.'

Martin gasped audibly. Did anybody still talk like that?

'We have our own ways,' said Mr Drogo. Martin had the idea that he was gently laughing at him.

Martin drove over to Willington in a fair state of resentment; he had had to lie to Sheila; had made up a story of church business and the offer of funds. It was the first time he'd ever seriously lied to her. But the whole business was so crazy . . . He'd tell her everything once he'd cleared it up.

The Drogo house was large, modern, but rather ugly,

standing well clear of its neighbours among mature decorative conifers. The granddaughter answered the door and took his coat.

'I'm the housekeeper tonight. It's the servants' night off.' Her appearance went with her voice; she was tall, about thirty, very much the confident businesswoman. Her looks could only be described as opulent: a mass of blue-black hair, swept up on top of her head, a figure that curved richly, but with the utmost discretion, in a dark-grey business suit with white lace at throat and wrists drawing attention to the plump, creamy beauty of her face and hands. No wedding ring. Her dark eyes surveyed him with a frank female interest that was disconcerting. It was the way certain rich men eyed a new woman . . . he flashed up in his mind a vision of Sheila, thin, red-haired and freckled. Ashamedly, he thought she made the vision of Sheila seem very thin indeed. She walked ahead of him, the powerful hips and calves moving discreetly, expensively, arrogantly.

The man who rose from the dark-red leather armchair could not possibly be the grandfather. He could be no more than fifty. The same blue-black hair and dark, amused eyes, the same sombre and wealthy solidness that could never be described as fat.

'Oh,' said Martin. 'I'd hoped to speak to Mr Drogo.'

'I *am* Mr Drogo.'

'Mr William Henry Drogo?'

'The same.'

'But . . .'

'Let me get you a drink. What will you have?' He moved to a highly polished mahogany sideboard. With its brass handles, Martin thought it looked like the most expensive kind of coffin. Desperately, he fought to get hold of himself. But his hand still trembled, and the sherry ran down over his fingers. For some reason he began to worry because he hadn't told Sheila exactly where he was going.

'Do sit down, Mr Williams. How can I help you?'

Martin glanced at the girl, sitting listening intently. She got up at once, saying, 'I must see to the dinner.' Fascinated, Martin watched her as she left the room. At his next confession, he was going to have to confess the sin of lechery. It was not a sin he had had to confess before.

'My granddaughter interests you.' It was not a question, it was a statement. There was no disapproval in it. Blindly, Martin lunged into the reason he had come: the phone call from the vanishing undertaker, the funeral of William Henry Drogo, booked a month ahead. Mr Drogo listened, nodding sympathetically, without a hint of surprise or disbelief. Martin finished up, lamely:

'I wouldn't have bothered you, only it's been preying on my mind. Is it just some ridiculous practical joke, or is it a – a threat of some kind? Against your life, or something? I mean, it sounds like something the Mafia would do – if we had anything like the Mafia in Muncaster.' He forced himself to smile and shrug at his own childishness.

'Oh,' said Mr Drogo. 'We *had* the Mafia in Muncaster, a couple of years ago. On a very small scale. They tried to take over an interest in one or two rather second-rate gambling clubs. Very small beer. We had a quiet word in the Chief Constable's ear, and they went away peacefully enough.'

The muffled note of a small dinner-gong echoed through the house. 'Come and eat,' said Mr Drogo, putting a fatherly hand on Martin's shoulder.

The meal was good, though a little strange and spicy. So was the wine. The daughter – no, the granddaughter – whose name was Celicia, moved about serving it as silently as a cat on the thick, red carpet. The rest of the time, from the side, she watched Martin as he talked. Or rather, listened.

Mr Drogo talked. In between eating with the most exquisite manners, he talked about Muncaster; he talked about St Austin's, right back to the time of the Augustinian canons. He talked with the authority of a historian. Martin was fascinated, the way he showed one thing growing out of another. He made it sound as if he'd lived right through it. Martin stopped trembling eventually. But if he listened to the grandfather, he secretly watched the girl. The girl watched him, too, a slight smile playing about the corners of her mouth.

'About that phone call.' Martin's voice, almost a shout, broke through the smooth flow of Mr Drogo's talk. 'Was I *meant* to come and tell you?'

'Yes, you were meant to come and tell me.' Mr Drogo pulled a grape from a bunch that lay on a dish near him and popped it into his mouth with evident enjoyment.

'But . . . *why*?'

'I am going to die – on March 26th.' He helped himself, unhurriedly, to another grape.

'Oh, I see. The doctor's told you. I'm so sorry.' Then reality broke in like a blizzard. 'But . . . but he can't have told you the exact date!'

'I chose the date.' Mr Drogo extracted a grape pip from the back of his excellent teeth, with the delicacy of a cat. He looked as healthy as any man Martin had ever seen.

'But what—'

'Do you know how old I am?' asked Mr Drogo. He might have been asking the right time. 'I am one hundred and ninety-two years old, on March 26th. I thought that made it rather neat.'

Martin stared wildly at the girl, as if assessing how much help she would be against this madman.

'And I am eighty-four next birthday,' said the girl. She smiled, showing all her perfect white teeth. Martin noticed that the canines were slightly, very slightly, longer than usual. But not more than many people's were . . .

Martin leapt to his feet, knocking over his chair behind him with a thud. 'I came here in good faith,' he cried. 'I didn't come here to be made a fool of!'

'We are not making a fool of you. Have you got your birth certificate, my dear?'

The girl disappeared into the hall, returning moments later with the certificate in her hand. She passed it across to Martin. Even now, in his rage and fear, her perfume was soothing . . . Hands trembling again, he unfolded the paper roughly, tearing it along one fold. It was old and frail and yellow.

Celicia Margaret Drogo. Born July 8th, 1887, To William Canzo Drogo and Margaret Drogo, formerly Betyl.

'Do you want to see her parents' marriage certificate?' asked Mr Drogo gently. 'I want your mind to be absolutely satisfied.'

'I'd like my coat,' shouted Martin, only half hoping he would be given it.

'As you wish,' said Mr Drogo. 'But,' he added, 'it would be easier for you if you went with my granddaughter now. She could make everything perfectly clear to you. She helped Canon Maitland to see things clearly. We gave Canon Maitland a very contented life for many years. He was almost one of us.'

'Get lost!' shouted Martin, most regrettably. 'All I want from you is my coat!'

They did not try to stop him. Celicia came with him, but only to help him on with his coat. Her fingers were still gentle, pleading, on the nape of his neck. Then he was outside and running for the car. He drove out of the drive like a lunatic, narrowly avoiding a collision with a Rover that hooted at him angrily until it turned a corner. He made himself pull up, then, and sit still till he had calmed down. Then he drove home shakily and painfully slowly. Sheila was just standing on the doorstep, pulling on her gloves before going to the pictures; she had a distaste for being in the rectory on her own at night and went to watch whatever film was on, however stupid.

'What's the matter with you?' She took him inside gently. After three whiskies, he plucked up the courage to tell her everything. It said a lot for her love for him that she believed him unquestioningly.

'I tried to ring you on Tuesday,' said the Bishop. 'Tried all day.'

'Tuesday's my day off,' said Martin. 'I was in London.'

'That explains it,' said the Bishop, who always had the last word, however pointless. He shuffled the papers on his desk, as if they were a squad of idle recruits. He had begun life as a major in the war, passed on to be an accountant, and only in later life been drawn to the church. Some spiteful clergy said he remained a major first, an accountant second and a bishop only third. His jutting nose and bristling moustache certainly sat oddly under his mitre on high days and holy days. Every church in his diocese had its accounts scrutinized by his eagle eye, and paid the uttermost farthing. He was brave, honest, loving and as unstoppable as one of his own old tanks when he'd made up his mind.

'I've taken up your complaint with Mr Drogo,' he announced. 'He apologized handsomely, I must say. Said his granddaughter was a great one for practical jokes, and rather a one for the men. More than I'd care to admit about *my* granddaughter. Said he was a fool to go along with her, but he didn't know how far she was going. Damned decent apology, I call that. He's writing to you. Wants you to take your missus over for a meal – make things up.'

Martin gaped. He had not complained about Mr Drogo; he had sent the Bishop a long and detailed report marked

Personal and Confidential. That Mr Drogo now knew all about it filled him with a nameless dread.

'It wasn't a practical joke,' he said. 'I've been doing some investigating. That's why I went to London – Somerset House: births, deaths and marriages. I spent the whole day checking. There has not been a single Drogo birth since 1887 – that *was* Celicia. But from the electoral rolls, there are at the present time thirty-two Drogos living in Muncaster.'

'Rubbish!' said the Bishop. 'Stuff and nonsense. Of course they were born – I know a lot of them well. Michael Drogo is solicitor to the diocesan board, Giles Drogo was chairman of Rotary last year. Why, in a quiet way, the Drogos *are* Muncaster. Don't know what we'd do without them. Without their generosity, St Austin's would have had to be demolished years ago. Your lectureship at the college is funded by Drogo money—'

'How long have *you* been in Muncaster?' shouted Martin. 'Ever baptized any Drogo babies?'

'I've been here five long years, my lad. And no, I've never baptized a Drogo baby – it's not my line of business. And what's more I won't have young clergymen who are no more than jacked-up curates havin' the vapours on *my* hearthrug. Go away, Martin, before I start revising my good opinion of you. You'll not prosper in Muncaster long if you get the Drogos' backs up. Though why anybody in their senses should want to . . . Stop waving those bits of paper in my face!' Colour was showing in the Bishop's cheeks – what the cathedral clergy referred to as the red warning flags.

'There's something funny going on at St Austin's . . . something against the will of God . . .'

'That,' said the Bishop, 'is my province to decide. If you don't agree with me, you can always resign. *Well?*'

Martin swallowed, and was silent, as the enormity of it hit him. If he resigned the living, Sheila and he had nowhere to go. They'd even sold off their own poor sticks of furniture, because they looked so pathetic in the opulence of the rectory. They could just about exist on Sheila's teaching salary, but if the Bishop passed the word he was an awkward hysterical character . . .

The Bishop pounced on his hesitation; he was never one to miss an opening. He came round the desk and put an arm on Martin's shoulder, in a way horribly reminiscent of Mr Drogo. 'This is racial prejudice, Martin, don't you see? There is foreign blood in the Drogos – touch of the tarbrush there, perhaps. Lot of people think they're Jews, but they're not. Good old Church of England – among our keenest supporters. They have their own funny ways in private, but they do a lot of damn good work in public. They don't do any *harm* – I happen to know their chemical workers are the highest-paid in the city. Live and let live, Martin, live and let live. Go home and think it over – I don't want to lose you now you're doing so well. Why, I've just had an invitation for you to give a talk on your city-centre work to the Social Science department of the university . . .' He picked up a thick, expensive-looking envelope from his desk, with the university crest on the back flap. 'Bless you, my boy.' He shook Martin's hand warmly on the way out.

Martin opened the envelope in the car, his hands shaking with something which might have been anticipation. There was the invitation to give the James Drogo Memorial Lecture.

On the twenty-eight of next month. Friday, 28th March. At 10.30 a.m.

'They want me out of the church on that morning,' gabbled Martin. 'Don't you see? They want me out of the way so they can . . .'

'Can what?' said Sheila, with a brave attempt at briskness. But her hand shook as she passed Martin another whisky.

'I don't know,' said Martin. 'That's the awful thing. It's only two weeks off and I don't *know*.'

'Well, they can hardly bury him in the churchyard. It's been closed how long? A hundred years?'

'More than that.'

'And it's so jam-packed it's practically standing-room only. And people would notice . . .'

'What people?' said Martin, despondently. 'Anyway, they wouldn't have to use the churchyard – St Austin's has got a crypt. All those names on plaques on the church walls – *near this spot lie the Mortal Remains of* etc. They're down under the floor in coffins on shelves, in a place probably as big as the church itself.'

'Ugh,' said Sheila. 'I didn't know that.'

'Most people don't, or they wouldn't go near some churches. It's a kind of clerical conspiracy of silence. What the eye doesn't see, the heart doesn't grieve over. Tastes have changed. Mind you, some crypts are just coke-holes, even headquarters for Telephone Samaritans or tramps' shelters, like St Martin-in-the-Fields. But a lot . . .'

Sheila glanced round the opulent kitchen and shuddered. 'Where was old Canon Maitland buried?'

'It'll be in the church diary – in the church. Let's go and look.'

Sheila glanced out of the kitchen window. Dusk was just starting to gather around the graceful spire of St Austin Friars.

'We can be there and back in ten minutes,' said Martin. 'It's better than wondering. Better than not knowing.'

The church door was locked, but Martin had his key. He banged his hand down across the massed banks of switches in the vestry and the whole church sprang out into light. Martin hoped the lights at this hour would not attract the eye of Mr Phillips. Old Phillips who knew the ropes, old Phillips who would see to it. Old Phillips who spent a quite extraordinary amount in the betting-shop for a poorly paid church verger.

They opened the church diary, holding their breath. The entry for the burial of William Henry Drogo, in Martin's own handwriting, mocked them.

'That was the *awful* thing,' whispered Martin. 'When he told me he was going to die, he smiled. As if he was looking forward it, like his summer holidays.'

Sheila firmly turned over the page in the book, because his own handwriting seemed to have paralysed Martin, like a snake hypnotizes a rabbit. The previous entry, in old Phillips' hand, recorded the funeral of Canon Maitland, conducted by a Revd Leonard Canzo, fellow of a minor Cambridge college. The body had been interred in . . .

. . . the crypt of St Austin Friars, by special faculty, authorized by the Bishop. Because of his long and faithful service to the church of seventy years . . .

'Where's the door down to the crypt?' whispered Sheila.

'I don't know. There are two I've never been down. One's the boiler-house for the central heating – I left all that to old Phillips.' They looked round nervously, expecting to see old Phillips coming up the aisle at any moment, in his dull overcoat and checked muffler, which he seemed to wear, winter and summer, as a uniform. But he was nowhere in sight. And yet all that stood between the brilliantly illuminated church and the verger's house was a flat stretch of demolition-site . . .

'Probably in the betting-shop,' said Sheila, and giggled, then stopped herself abruptly.

They swiftly found the pair of doors; the door-surrounds were Gothic and crumbling, but the doors were Victorian, oak and very solid. And the hasps and padlocks on them were even newer and even more solid.

'Have you got keys?'

'Not for these locks.'

'Old Phillips has got them,' said Sheila grimly. She

thought. 'Look, most boiler-rooms have another door to the outside, for the coke-deliveries in the old days – I mean, they didn't want coke all over the aisle floors and people crunching up to communion. That might be open – it's worth a try.'

Every fibre of his body said no. But some kind of frenetic excitement had seized Sheila. She flew off down the aisle. He didn't dare wait to switch the lights off; besides, they would need them, shining out through the church windows, if they were not to break a leg in the wilderness of tilted table-tombs, leaning urns and tangled brambles in the graveyard outside. He wished he'd thought to bring a torch . . . but he caught sight of Sheila's slim figure, in her white mac, flitting through the tomb-scape ahead. Halfway round, he found her waiting for him, outside a low Gothic door.

'It's shut,' she said. 'Locked.'

He felt suddenly flat, and yet glad. 'It'll only be the coke-hole,' he said. In the semi-dark, they could hear the coke-droppings of centuries crunching beneath their feet. Relief made him gabby. 'It's funny about this churchyard; disused urban churchyards are usually a menace: vandals writing on the tombs with aerosols, or throwing the gravestones over – even black magic cranks. But here, there isn't a trace of vandalism—'

A hand on his arm stopped him both talking and walking. She pointed ahead. There was a faint crunching of footsteps on the coky path. 'Somebody's coming.' They hid in a flurry behind a miniature Greek temple, black as coal.

It was old Phillips, shabby overcoat and checked muffler. He kept glancing up at the lighted windows of the church as he walked; a little uneasy, a little cautious. He passed, and went as far as the locked door. Without benefit of torch or light, he fitted a key neatly first time into the keyhole.

'That's not the first time he's done that in the dark,' whispered Sheila.

'Shhh!'

Old Phillips swung the door open; the hinges did not creak.

'Well-oiled,' muttered Sheila.

'*Shhh!* What's he doing?'

But it was all too obvious what old Phillips was doing. He was returning, leaving the little door not only unlocked but ajar. He passed again, and faded into the dusk.

'What's he done that for?' whispered Sheila. 'That's mad – *unlocking* a door at dusk. Shall we look inside?'

Just then, the church windows above their heads went dark. Old Phillips was busy putting off the church lights. Another light went off, and another. It was enough to panic them. They fled across the graveyard, and didn't stop running till they reached the rectory.

'Quick!' said Martin. 'Let's get all the lights on – on the *far* side of the house. Not these. Phillips can see these from the church.' Suddenly it was desperately important that Phillips should not know they'd been anywhere near the church.

They went and sat in the sitting room, which, fortunately, *was* on the side away from the church. The central heating was on, but low, and the room was too cold. Martin banged on all three bars of the electric fire and the telly. They sat shivering till the room began to warm up. 'Get something to do,' whispered Martin, savagely. 'Get your knitting out. Take your coat off. Get your slippers on . . .' He was just taking off his own coat and hiding it behind the settee, when there came a ring on the doorbell. 'Relax!' screeched Martin, and made himself walk slowly to answer it.

Old Phillips' face was set in that look of joyful censoriousness beloved of caretakers the world over. He held up Martin's bunch of keys.

'Your keys, I believe, Mr Williams. I found the church unlocked and *all* the lights on. Vestry open, *and* the church diary.' He held that up in turn, still open at the page that recorded Canon Maitland's funeral. 'I thought at first it was vandals.'

'Sorry,' said Martin, and his voice didn't shake. 'I've been meaning to go back and lock up, but I got lost in the football on telly. Won't you come in for a moment? The match is just over.'

Phillips came in; his eyes did not miss the slippers and the knitting, the telly and the warmth of the room. They roamed over everything, making it dirty as if they were a pair of grey slugs. When he was satisfied, *barely* satisfied, he turned to them.

'You want to be careful, Mr Williams. A lot more careful. And you, Mrs Williams. Canon Maitland would never have made a mistake like that. Very happy and well-settled here, Canon Maitland was.'

They all knew he wasn't talking about the church keys.

They were careful. They hardly went near the church at all; Martin found he could no longer face his solo Wednesday service. If God was listening above, who was listening down below, beneath the black stone slabs of the nave floor? Martin found his thoughts going downward far more than they ever ascended upward. What was down there? Why did they need their door *opened* at dusk? What was Mr Drogo looking forward to, more than his holidays? Anyway, old Phillips was now round the place practically every hour of the day and night, as the 28th of March approached. None of the crypt doors was ever found unlocked again.

But they planned carefully, too, for the 28th of March; and it worked out well. An actor friend called Larry Harper stayed in the rectory overnight (and they were very glad to have him). He was tall, thin and fair like Martin, and by the time he had donned Martin's rector's garb and a huge pair of horn-rimmed spectacles, he even gave Sheila a fright. His walk was the living image of Martin's lope; he said he'd been practising mimicking it for nearly a year, to get a laugh round The Grapes.

He left for the university at nine-thirty, Sheila with him in her best suit and hat, driving the car. He delivered Martin's talk (from the pages Martin had written out for him) far more convincingly than Martin would ever have done, and got a tremendous round of applause. He fumbled his impromptu question-time rather badly, but everyone put that down to well-earned exhaustion. Nobody at the university ever dreamed they hadn't seen the real Martin Williams . . .

. . . Who had been up the tower of St Austin Friars since seven that morning, creeping in through the cobwebbed dewiness of the graveyard with a sergeant from Muncaster Constabulary, summoned by phone with some nasty hints of black-magic activity in the churchyard. They waited behind the uppermost parapet of the tower, well-hidden, so that they saw it all.

At ten-twenty, the overcoated, mufflered figure of old Phillips walked leisurely through the churchyard and unlocked the main door. At ten-twenty-five he began to toll the bell. At ten-twenty-eight, five large black Rolls-Royce limousines started across the huge demolition-plain, following a Rolls-Royce hearse. Thirty-one Drogos, men and women, emerged, sleek in black top-coats, black fur coats and the flash of a black-nyloned leg. All the women were very handsome and looked about thirty, so it was impossible to pick Celicia out. There was the undertaker, Mr Betyl, no doubt, proper in black tail-coat and top-hat swathed in black muslin. The opulent coffin (which looked sickeningly like Mr Drogo's sideboard) vanished into the church.

'Let's go and get a good view inside,' Martin whispered to the sergeant. They went down through the bell-chamber –

the bell had stopped tolling but was still swaying in its bed – and down into the ringers' chamber, where a little window gave a good view into the body of the church, from just under the ancient rafters.

Martin looked down, and almost fainted.

Far from a scattering of thirty-one Drogos near the front, the church was full. The door to the crypt was gaping open. And as he looked down, every dark figure turned and looked up at him.

'Come on down, Mr Williams,' called Betyl, the undertaker, with sepulchral joviality. 'We are so glad you could make it after all.'

Martin turned desperately to the policeman.

'Time to go, sir,' said the policeman gently. He got out his warrant card and held it up open for Martin to inspect.

Sergeant Harold Morsk, Muncaster CID.

Like a condemned man, Martin tottered down the stairs and was marched to the front of the congregation.

'We shall only require you to say amen,' said Mr Betyl. 'We are a god-fearing race and have always supported your church. It is the least you can do for us.' Then he began to declaim to the congregation in a harsh, strange tongue, and they replied in the same tongue. And when they all looked at Martin with their smooth, handsome faces, he knew it was time to say, 'Amen.' Twice, they took black books from their pockets and broke out into a hymn. Old Phillips played the organ reasonably well. Then the body was reverently borne, on the shoulders of six pall-bearers, down into the crypt. One corner, grating against the door-jamb, lost a sliver of wood and rich varnish, and some flakes of white limestone dropped on the black floor.

After all was over down there (strange sounds floated up in the silence above) a man who looked incredibly like the late William Henry Drogo came across to Martin and shook him firmly and warmly by the hand.

'I am glad you were here. If *they* are not blessed by the presence of a clergyman, they get out of hand and run wild, and then there is trouble. There are still people cruel enough to sharpen ash-stakes for us – the world gets little better, except on the surface. Now we shall have no trouble in Muncaster . . . thank you.' He paused, and said concernedly, 'You do not look well . . . these things are troubling you . . . you may have bad dreams. Here is my granddaughter – Celicia, come here, Celicia – she has an affection for you. Go with her now, and she will make all things well and clear for you. No, Celicia, *not* in the crypt – the vestry will do for Mr Williams.' He spoke to her quite sharply, as if he suddenly feared she might go too far.

As in a dream, Martin walked through the open vestry door, his hand in Celicia's.

When he woke up on the vestry floor, he could never quite remember anything that had happened the morning of the 28th of March, in the church of St Austin Friars.

But it didn't matter, for shortly afterwards he and Sheila left the city, for a small rural living that had fallen vacant in Kent.

SERGEANT NICE

Constable William Bainbridge was enough to make a super-intendent tear his hair; a cause of premature balding, a breeder of peptic ulcers.

He had *some* virtues. He was never caught with long hair showing down his neck, under the rim of his uniform cap, like some. He was never caught with the bottom of his pullover showing below his tunic, like others. Ten years' service with the Royal Engineers had seen to that. And he was well liked on his beat. He never parked his Panda up a cul-de-sac and wasted his time chewing toffees. He got out and met the people; played for his village football team, coached the youngsters and never let them call him Bill in uniform. People didn't give a guilty start when they saw him sitting behind the counter in the off-licence, drinking a mug of tea.

But he was too soft to make a copper. There was the matter of the police station cat, which formed the habit of bringing home live earthworms. Most coppers ignored the worms, trampling them into pink rags on the parquet floor. Bill went to infinite bother to rescue them on a piece of paper, carrying them carefully back to the nearest verge. One day, so engaged, he met Super Green coming in.

'Has the worm turned at last, Bainbridge?' Then Super Green saw the worm was being borne aloft on a clean piece of his own official notepaper.

Or the time Bill hit a blackbird while proceeding in his Panda. Only Bill would have bothered to park and go back to render aid. He parked, not illegally, but inconveniently. One juggernaut, passing, scraped a yard of paint off another. The blackbird, rescued, not only recovered but showed Bill its gratitude by crapping all over the back of the Panda and the shoulder of Bill's best uniform tunic. After that, whenever the crafty old club comedians asked whose name they should mention, to get a laugh at the annual Police Social, people said 'Bainbridge and the blackbird'.

Worse, he had never made an arrest, or even reported anybody, in five years' service. Not that, in his area, there was much to report. Farmers hurrying the harvest home after dusk without rear lights. Bill had a quiet word. A flurry of pale, shapely legs in a car parked in a public place after dark. Bill walked past, whistling loudly. Came back once the flurry had subsided and tapped on the window till it was wound down. Talked to the lady a minute, then pointed out the time and passed blithely on. No need to upset people, make enemies.

Crime in his district stayed low. Super Green said that the people on his beat went elsewhere to commit their offences, rather than hurt his feelings. Chief Super Higginson called his beat 'the bird sanctuary', because nobody on it was doing bird.

Meanwhile, Bill flung himself into being a good citizen. He was often to be found in the primary school, with his little talks on the Green Cross Code, his Cycling Proficiency Tests, his tactful lectures on why you shouldn't take sweeties from strange men. And he was often accompanied by the photographer from the local paper, which was chronically short of news. It usually ended up with a close-up of Bill holding a fetching infant in his arms. He had a weakness for that, probably because he'd never had any kids of his own. Finally, the paper headlined him as *Oldcastle Constabulary's Mr Nice*, and after that he was always known around the police station as 'Constable Nice'.

The superintendents nearly had a fit. They thought of getting rid of him, until he rescued from drowning two children who had tried to walk on the water at the local sewage farm. 'I see Bainbridge is in the shit again,' said Super Green. But it wasn't really funny; especially when the Royal Humane Society gave him a certificate for it. 'Now he's got a certificate to prove he's human,' said Super Green. 'Humane,' corrected Chief Super Higginson, a grate in his voice.

Bill tried to get on even with the police. A keen photographer, he was much in demand at the annual Police Ball. He even made a home-movie of the police scoring the winning goal in the Oldcastle Sunday League Cup. And if someone was put in hospital by the yobbish supporters of Oldcastle United, it was Bill who organized the whip-round and called at the hospital with the basket of fruit. He even designed and built a delta-winged, petrol-engined, radio-controlled model aircraft for Super Green's son's birthday (though he was paid for the materials). It was not Bill's fault that the child let the plane fly too high, get out of control and nose-dive up to its tail in a neighbour's lawn, missing the unhappy gardener by inches.

But it was his bid for promotion that was the last straw. Bill had a fair number of O and A levels, acquired by correspondence course during long winter evenings in the army. He sat, and passed, the police exam for sergeant. Then, ludicrously, he applied to take the exam for inspector.

'He's after my job,' said Super Green. 'Or yours.' Chief Super Higginson laughed.

But the Chief Constable of the County didn't find it funny at all. The police, he informed them by letter, was supposed to be a satisfying career, in which bright and eager constables could expect promotion . . .

'We could make him desk-sergeant,' said Super Green.

'The drunks would run rings round him.'

'What about the crime computer?'

'He wouldn't believe half the nasty things it told him.'

'I know, what about the Boob Patrol?'

The two Supers became so pleased with themselves, they actually got the whisky out of the filing cabinet marked *Traffic Statistics 1945–60*.

If you were an old copper or a scared copper or a useless copper, you were either put on Schools' Road Safety or the Boob Patrol, which meant the sea front at Graymouth. Graymouth prided itself on being a family resort; it had taken a pounding recently from package holidays, but kept going bravely. When Oldcastle Council failed to paint the sea-front railings because of the cuts, the locals formed a committee and painted them themselves. That kind of town.

The local police station in Front Street was combined with a sergeant's house, complete with noticeboard in the garden carrying faded warnings about rabies and colorado beetle. The duties of the three daytime constables comprised placating howling lost children, directing old ladies to the toilets and getting the holiday traffic parked in the morning and out in the evening. Otherwise, you could watch the sea birds, the tide coming in or going out, and the endless stream of young, brown female flesh drifting up Front Street from the beach, barefoot and licking ice-cream cones. Hence, the Boob Patrol.

Sergeant Nice, as he was now known, moved with his big, raw-boned, comfortable wife into the police station. He spent most of that wet spring having quiet words with tramps occupying beach huts and laying the foundations of a huge floral display in the sloping police-station garden. When it bloomed in early summer, this turned out to be a ten-foot replica, in white alyssum and blue lobelia, of the county police badge, accompanied by the legend *Oldcastle*

Constabulery. The local paper photographed it (and Sergeant Nice) in colour. The sergeant was quoted as saying that Graymouth was a family resort, which must be kept safe for the kiddies; and promising ruthless war on unlicensed and extortionate popcorn-sellers and topless bathers. The Supers were not amused, until they spotted the spelling mistake in *Constabulery* and made Sergeant Nice do his corrections with a gardening trowel.

But only high summer exposed Sergeant Nice's real plans for Graymouth. He had scrounged white cap-covers out of Traffic Department stores for his three constables' caps; white point-duty gloves too. Tunics were abandoned early; shirt sleeves were rolled immaculately just above the elbow, shoes polished like black diamonds, and the morale of the Boob Patrol boosted sky high. Not least by a large new beach hut, funded by the Rotary and manned by some very pretty college girls. It had a wooden sign on the roof which read LOST CHILDREN one side, and HOLIDAY INFORMATION the other. One wall sported two ancient lifebelts, newly painted in red and white, another a huge hand-painted map of Graymouth showing every item of interest from the Egyptian Gardens to the Victoria Jubilee Clocktower and Drinking Fountain. All these things had been personally painted by Sergeant Nice himself, who told the local paper, 'A contented public is a law-abiding public.'

Only two other things of note happened that first summer. There was an outbreak of pick-pocketing in the amusement arcade that proved impossible to solve because Sergeant Nice wouldn't stay away from the place half an hour. In the end, he was put on a compulsory first aid course to get him out of the way, and a plain-clothesman from Oldcastle caught the thief two hours later. And, rather more worrying, a flasher was reported by two teenage girls in the north beach shelter. Sergeant Nice half strangled him, tearing his shirt in two places. The flasher muttered about complaining to his lawyer, but settled for the price of a new shirt.

At the end of four months, the Supers looked at each other and sighed.

'It could have been a lot worse,' said Super Green.

'Let sleeping dogs lie,' said Chief Super Higginson. 'Graymouth Rotary actually seem to like him . . .'

The trouble started by the Victoria Jubilee Clocktower and Drinking Fountain. Stolen beach-bag. The woman had put it down on the fountain while she got sand out of her shoes. When she put her hand out to retrieve it, it was simply no longer there. There had been a lot of people about, but nobody had seen anything. For the simple reason that at that very moment, something had gone wrong with one of Front Street's lamps. An elaborate cast-iron Gothic affair of the type beloved of seaside resorts, it had suffered some kind of short circuit and blown an impressive stream of blue-white sparks over the passing cars. Nobody had been hurt, but there had been a good deal of commotion, and when the woman turned back for her bag, it was gone.

Sergeant Nice gave her and her husband a cup of tea and took down particulars of what had been stolen. Beach-bag, green striped. Handbag, black plastic. Fifty pounds in five pound notes. The family insurance policies. Camera full of holiday snaps. Three small presents for the grandchildren back home in Plymouth. The couple were not well off; they would have to return home early. The woman was white with the shock that follows theft, and her husband was tight-lipped. Twice, the woman cried. The ruins of a lovely holiday. Sergeant Nice felt hatred for the thief and offered to lend the couple ten pounds of his own money. They refused. Sergeant Nice wondered whether he could get the Rotary to start a fund for this sort of thing.

The woman insisted on showing him exactly how it had happened. Just to comfort her, Sergeant Nice went along.

The Victoria Jubilee Clocktower was a notable monstrosity, in that shiny, pink-brown stone that has fossils embedded in it. It was topped by a corroded weathervane that no longer turned. Below a roof like a mini Greek temple, the four clock faces all told slightly different times, except the one that was broken. Beneath those was a riot of buttresses, gargoyles and marble owls, down to the drinking fountain that dribbled water endlessly into a foul black marble bowl that appeared to be full of growing seaweed. There was a pint-sized bronze drinking cup attached to the fountain by a chain that could have anchored a battleship, which even vandals couldn't vandalize. The cup was also so black inside that no one had drunk from it in living memory. The whole erection had been the overriding delightful horror of Sergeant Nice's childhood trips to Graymouth. It still fascinated him; he wondered if he could persuade the Rotary to restore it to its former splendour.

But none of this interested the woman. She led him round behind, to a low coffin-like object in the same pink fossilized stone. A horse trough, so the bronze plaque informed, given to celebrate the accession of King Edward VII and for the refreshment of four-footed friends. It would have refreshed no four-footed friends now, even had one been present. Its inside was dry and dusty as an Egyptian tomb, with a couple of lolly-sticks and a crumpled crisp bag. Inside this, the woman said, she had dumped her beach-bag. For safety.

Sergeant Nice pushed back his uniform cap and scratched his crinkly ginger hair in a way that would not have been approved of by the Supers. The horse trough puzzled him. He did not remember ever having seen it before. Instead, from childhood, he seemed to recall a round manhole cover set into the road, emblazoned *Sewer Lid. J. Holcraft & Co, Sheffield.*

Patent pending. Right under where the horse trough now stood. Yes, he was sure, because the sewer lid had been surrounded by a circular pattern of ornamental cobbles. And part of that circular pattern was still there, vanishing under the horse trough. But who on earth would have installed a horse trough since Sergeant Nice's childhood? Since 1955, Graymouth couldn't have had a carthorse to bless itself with . . .

'I don't believe you've heard a word I've been saying,' said the woman, crossly.

'Sorry, madam. Wool-gathering.'

The couple left soon after, the husband saying bitterly, 'Reckon you've seen the last o' your bag. Right ninnies the police put on these seaside beats.'

Hurt but persistent, Sergeant Nice continued to examine the horse trough. He made a forlorn attempt to lift it; it must have weighed several tons. He inspected the place where it joined the clocktower proper; there was no visible new join, it all seemed of a piece. He re-read the plaque. The trough had been presented by Alderman G. G. Sharratt and the date was 1902. Sergeant Nice had an uncomfortable feeling that if he went on investigating the horse trough, it would end up as another good laugh at the Police Social. But he was a slow, stubborn man. He went across and consulted young Thomas, the newsagent, bearded purveyor of whirling celluloid windmills, inferior buckets and spades from Hong Kong and paperbacks of near-nude girls sporting black thigh boots and Luger pistols.

'Dunno,' said young Thomas, combing his beard with his fingers. 'I've only been here five years. You get so used to seeing things like that, you don't notice.'

Then two worried strangers came hurrying across dragging a screaming lost child.

*

The next thing to be pinched was an expensive Japanese camera. The victim, a college lecturer, had only put it down in the horse trough for a second, while he got out his telephoto lens. Then a fat lady had collapsed against him, come over all faint in the heat. By the time he'd got her to a bench, the camera was gone.

'Where's this fat lady now?' asked Sergeant Nice. 'Bet we won't see hide nor hair of *her* again.' The thief could not have picked a better accomplice to act as decoy.

But when they reached the scene of crime, the fat lady was still there, only partially recovered and surrounded by husband, five children, an aged aunt and the family from next door. No sneak-thief could afford to pay eleven decoys; especially as they gave local addresses which they were quite eager to have checked.

The third victim of theft, the same evening, was a young girl who had lost a wet bathing-costume wrapped in a sandy towel. Just put it down in the horse trough while she ran a comb through her long wet blonde hair. Her attention had been distracted when two cars collided at low speed, strewing the road with headlamp-glass.

Sergeant Nice's head began to whirl. What kind of nut steals a camera one hour and a wet bathing-costume the next? What kind of nut uses the same modus operandi, in the same spot, three times running on the same day? Come to that, what kind of nut can make fat ladies faint, cars crash and street lamps short-circuit? I'm getting a touch of the sun myself, he thought, setting his white-topped cap more firmly on his head. He wouldn't dare breathe a word of this, or he *would* get mentioned at the next Police Social. Then he sighed with relief. It's all coincidence. People faint every day, cars crash, street lamps short-circuit. What's new about this joker is that he waits for these things to happen, then takes advantage. Simple, really. Quite clever.

So when the constables reported in at the end of the day, he questioned them closely about funny, non-criminal incidents that had made people stare. The constables screwed up their faces. Like what, Sarge? He tried to explain, then had to turn away for a moment, to answer the phone. When he turned back, the constables were nudging each other, and they had a lot of trouble getting their faces straight again. Sergeant Nice had to be downright nasty in the end, to preserve discipline. Their gossip would be all over Oldcastle police canteen by tomorrow.

Still, they were able to report no unusual incidents that day, anywhere else but the clocktower. Nothing more unusual than women belting screaming kids, or young men sliding their hands down the backs of their girlfriends' bathing-costumes. And those things happened every day in Graymouth in the season.

I must be getting paranoid in my old age, thought Sergeant Nice as he got into his striped pyjamas ready for bed. He was proud of knowing what 'paranoid' meant. Few of his colleagues did.

The following morning, council electricians came to repair the street light. Came grumbling. Why couldn't Graymouth wait its turn in the queue? There were broken street lights all over the Oldcastle district. But this bugger in his white-topped cap, who thought he was God Almighty, had rung up their boss and disrupted their comfy work-schedule, demanding that they see to it *immediately*, because it might be a danger to the public.

Sergeant Nice slipped them a quid, in return for a detailed report on what had gone wrong with the lamp. This softened them; but they started giving him funny looks. OK, they giggled, as they were borne aloft on their yellow telescopic working-platform. Why mock the afflicted? A quid was a quid; a drink was a drink. Sergeant Nice knew what they were saying, but his back was broad.

They came across to the police station two hours later, sweating with effort and with a different look on their faces. They had never seen anything like it. Wire and junction-box were burnt right out – like arc-welding. Newly installed wire it had been, too, not a year old. And a brand new junction-box. Should have had a five-year life at least. Perhaps the moisture in the sea air?

'It was early afternoon,' said Sergeant Nice. 'Boiling hot sunshine all day. And we haven't had rain for a week. So where's the moisture coming from?'

They shrugged. They had never seen anything like it, they repeated; but those lamps were old. They'd have been scrapped years ago, anywhere else but Graymouth.

'It hadn't been nobbled?' asked Sergeant Nice.

'Nobbled?'

'Got at?' He didn't want to say the word, but in the end he had to. 'Sabotaged?'

No chance of sabotage, they said. Why, they'd been an hour unscrewing things to get at the fault. The only other way – the power supply – would have blown every lamp in the street. Anyway, who'd want to sabotage a street lamp? Funny looks and nudges again. Now his name would be all over the council workmen's canteen too.

He brooded so much over his lunch that his wife came to the conclusion that she needn't have bothered cooking. Nothing ever actually stopped him eating; he liked his grub too much for that. But in this mood he'd eat baked beans on toast and never notice.

He brooded about gossip. Not gossip about himself, but gossip that would harm the good name of the town. God knew, times were hard enough for the shopkeepers without *this*. One day-tripper with a grievance could put off ten more from coming. Graymouth was becoming the place where you got your handbag pinched. People needed to be carefree on holiday; towels, trannies, picnic baskets left unattended all over the beach. If you couldn't be a bit careless on holiday, when could you be? This johnny would have to be dealt with, quick.

Simple enough. Watch the clocktower like a hawk from young Thomas's shop. The moment something funny began happening, head for the horse trough.

But it wasn't quite that simple. Young Thomas didn't mind him settling behind the fridge, staring out at the clocktower between two rows of nuddy-magazines hanging up outside the window. But the public minded. Even though he didn't look round when they came in, he could feel their glances on the back of his neck, the sudden cautious muting of their voices. They hurried through their purchases; couldn't wait to get out of the shop. Bought less than they would have done. Nobody loves a copper. He was ruining young Thomas's trade. Worse, people would be talking about him, speculating about what he was up to. Sooner or later, the sneak-thief would overhear.

He went home and changed into khaki slacks and a beach shirt. He even opened the fridge for Thomas and handed out the correct number of raspberry lollies. Pretended to read a nuddy-magazine, full of girls who looked like pink plastic dolls, untouched by human hand. For the holiday-makers, he faded into the background. But the locals began to notice and make snide remarks about moonlighting and the police being poorly paid. And his own constables kept bringing him trivial matters, with stupid smirks on their faces. Still, he was a patient man.

At twenty past four, his patience paid off. Two dogs started a fight. Quite small dogs, but the howling and snarling sounded like murder at the zoo. In a second, Sergeant Nice had vaulted the fridge, knocked down a revolving rack of picture-postcards, caught it on the wing, handed it to an amazed woman customer and was running into the street, straight for the horse trough. This time . . .

There was a continuous desperate tooting from his right. It was as well he looked. An old Morris Minor, headlights blazing in the afternoon sunlight, was swerving wildly through scattering holiday-makers at a terrifying speed. Sergeant Nice leapt for his life, ending up with his face and palms embedded with the gravel of the road. He had just time to notice he'd torn the knee out of his slacks when there was a shrill screaming of brakes and a tremendous crash of glass from the sea end of Front Street. He turned to see the Morris Minor with its nose wedged in the glass skylights over the underground public lavatory, and a stream of men, like provoked soldier ants, issuing from the lavatory stairs, alternately trying to comb glass out of their hair and do up the flies of their trousers. One, hopping like a kangaroo with his trousers round his ankles, obviously had more serious problems.

But first things first. Sergeant Nice ran on for the horse trough, leaving the flying uniformed figure of Constable Hughes to take charge of things at the sanitation end.

When he reached the clocktower, everyone was still watching the scene round the Morris Minor.

'Anyone lost anything?' he shouted. 'Anybody had anything stolen?'

The holiday-makers didn't understand at first; stared at him as if he was mad. Then a woman began that desperate looking round, that one pace forward and another back, that agitated moving of the hands and searching the already-searched that could only mean one thing.

'Me handbag,' she said, hand going to her plump throat. 'I just put it down there for a moment . . .'

The dry, empty bottom of the horse trough leered up at Sergeant Nice.

'Tell us again how it happened,' said Sergeant Nice.

The driver of the Morris Minor could not have looked less criminal. He was only five foot three, with a Beatle haircut, large, sad, brown eyes and the wizened air of a retired jockey. He was accompanied by a wife and five kids, who testified steadily and vociferously to the truth of everything she said.

'Oi've never done more than fifty in me loif.' Shock had made the Brummy accent very strong. 'The owld car won't do more than fifty; she's a toired old girl. Oi was looking for a place to park when it 'appened. She suddenly went *mad*.'

'I'm glad you had the presence of mind to put on your headlights and sound your horn.' Sergeant Nice felt entitled to a tiny sarcasm.

'*Oi* didn't switch the loits on. Moi 'and was nowhere near the 'orn.'

'It wasn't neither,' said his wife. ''E just sat there, scared paraloised.'

'Moi foot was nowhere near the accelerator neither. Oi had it on the broik, but it weren't working. The car just seemed to go *mad*!'

'The brakes worked in the end. Just before you hit the public lavatory.'

'Oi know – that's the funny thing. That's just what Oi said to Ingrid 'ere. Oi'm not driving that thing again – it can go to the scrapheap. And it only passed its MOT last week . . .'

In the end, they were very hard to get rid of. They sat around staring at Sergeant Nice as if he owed them some explanation. As they finally left the station, he could still hear the little Brummy's voice raised in querulous indignation. 'It just seemed to go mad . . .'

Sergeant Nice drew out a spotless white hanky and wiped

his brow. He had done all he could. The man had been breathalysed; stone cold sober, his breath reeking of chips with vinegar bought further up the coast. The car had been sent to a garage to await the vehicle examiner, but the sergeant had a nasty feeling that it would be found fault-free, except for half a public lavatory skylight in the treads of its front tyres.

The dogs, it seemed, had finished their quarrel and vanished, in the very moment the car crash started. Nobody had noticed them again. The woman's handbag had contained seventy-seven pounds in cash, a chequebook and cheque card.

Sergeant Nice decided to interview the two drivers involved in yesterday's collision.

'Well, all I can say is that the manhole cover *should* be there,' said the man from the council, crossly. 'It's marked quite clearly on the plan. I mean, if this stretch of sewer got blocked, or fell in, things could get really nasty. We'd have to get down into it from the next manhole cover in St George's Road, and that's two hundred yards – and that's a hell of a walk underground. I mean, this is a main sewer. Mind you, we do have trouble with manholes getting covered up – mainly by the country road maintenance lot. They'll tarmac over a manhole cover as soon as look at you. Then the water board find out, and *we* cop it in the neck.'

'There used to be a manhole cover here,' said Sergeant Nice. 'I remember it as a little lad. Made by J. Holcraft and Co., Sheffield. And look, you can still see the ornamental cobbles that surrounded it.'

'You don't have to tell me,' said the man from the council. 'I've got eyes.'

'When would it last have been inspected?'

The man from the council gave him a curious look. 'We don't *inspect* them. We haven't got the manpower to go round inspecting covers like that. We never know till the water board needs them, and then they complain and we get it in the neck.'

'It would have been . . . noticed since 1902?'

'What's 1902 got to do with it?' said the man from the council, suspiciously.

Sergeant Nice tapped the bronze date on the horse trough. This seemed to incense the man from the council.

''Course it will have been noticed. This sewer was totally refurbished in 1936 – it would have got new manhole covers then. There'll have been men down this manhole a dozen times since then . . . we're not idle, you know.' He glared at Sergeant Nice. 'Though what interest it is to you . . .'

He drove away finally in his new Ford Fiesta, vowing there would be trouble soon and implying it was all Sergeant Nice's fault.

'There were two phone calls while you were out,' said Sergeant Nice's wife. 'One from the Chief Environment Health Officer and one from the Head of Traffic Police. They were both sorry you were out. Seemed to want to tell you to mind your own business and stop interfering with their departments. They're both going to ring back. What bee have you got in your bonnet now?' Sergeant Nice grunted, but didn't bother to reply. Deep in thought, he was forking a lunch of baked beans on toast into his mouth. Three incidents in one minute were too much to stomach. Two dogs fighting (though the Oldcastle police would not strictly regard that as an incident), a highly dangerous car crash and the theft of a handbag. All occurring within fifty yards of the clocktower. And no other incidents reported that day in Graymouth at all, except a late-night fight behind the Priory Arms, two domestics and a slot machine broken into. And they were all routine.

What the hell was going on round the clocktower? What kind of criminal could set two dogs fighting, make a perfectly sound (and still perfectly sound) car go berserk in the hands of a timid, sober driver with a car load of little kids? Sergeant Nice delved into the depths of his knowledge. A conjurer – the quickness of the hand deceives the eye? Mass-hypnosis, which was supposed to lie at the bottom of the Indian Rope Trick? Sergeant Nice pulled himself back to reality sharply.

But two things were clear. Somebody (call him X) was stealing a wildly differing series of things from that horse trough. And X would go to the lengths of endangering life to make sure he was not observed. If two dogs fighting was not enough to bamboozle the police, then a crashing car was added. A pretty ruthless villain . . . Or was he? No lives had been lost. No serious injury. But there might have been.

Somehow, Sergeant Nice just knew that any attempt by a living copper to catch the thief red-handed would be met with yet another bizarre distraction. Which would succeed. There had to be another way . . . Suddenly, Sergeant Nice knew the answer. He began to chuckle to himself, then came right out of his dark mood. He pushed the rest of his lunch aside.

'You know I can't stand baked beans.'

'Welcome home,' said his wife, sarcastically.

Young Thomas didn't mind having a cine-camera in his upstairs front bedroom. He didn't even mind having a control-wire running down his stairs, to a control-box beside his till.

'If anything starts in the street outside,' said Sergeant Nice, 'just press that button and it'll start the camera.'

'What do you mean, anything?' asked Thomas.

'Anything that would make you run to your shop door to watch. Like that street lamp blowing up, or two dogs fighting . . .'

'Whatever turns you on,' said Thomas. 'But I wish you'd tell me what it's all about. The wife's being difficult, she says she always cleans the bedroom on Wednesdays; *and* we can't draw the bedroom curtains properly.'

'I want to get film of that guy who's lifting handbags.'

'Keen,' said Thomas. 'Good as *Kojak*. Better than *Kojak*. Don't use real policemen, use a newsagent – save the government money. The Chancellor'd love you.'

'Be a good lad,' said Sergeant Nice, coaxingly.

'Does the Super know about this?' Then Thomas looked sympathetic and said, 'OK. I won't split on you. I'll leave that to the wife. I reckon she'll take three days of it before she rings the Super.'

It took two days to work. Two whole, sunny days of total peace and quiet which drove Sergeant Nice to despair. Then, on the third morning, it happened. Another street light blew, even more spectacularly. There was a fair crowd round the clocktower at the time: motorbikers. They liked the firework display a lot. Danced wildly up and down trying to catch the glinting sparks as they showered down. When the party was over, they discovered they had lost six crash helmets and four pairs of real leather gauntlets. All of which had been piled, for safety, inside the horse trough. Sergeant Nice was a quarter of a mile away at the time. He had been forcing himself to move further and further away from the clocktower for two whole days; it had required great moral courage.

But Thomas was jubilant. 'I pressed your button. We've got it – him, I mean.'

Sergeant Nice walked upstairs prudently, taking care not to hope for too much. Yes, the cine-camera on its tripod was still pointing in the right direction. Young Thomas's wife hadn't disturbed it in her cleaning or curtain-pulling. The 500 mm telephoto lens still enclosed a generous view of the clock-tower. The electronic exposure meter was working, focus was perfect. The whole four minutes of film was used up, run through. Allowing himself moderate hope, Sergeant Nice removed the film from the camera.

'Going to have it processed in the police lab?' asked young Thomas eagerly.

Sergeant Nice thought of the comedians at the Police Social, and shook his head.

'I can get it done for you,' said Thomas. 'Cheap. Twenty-four-hour service. I'll run it up in the car myself. I know a guy through the camera club.'

Sergeant Nice frowned. He had no great opinion of the guys Thomas knew. Most of them sold Thomas things like duff Hong Kong tape recorders at ridiculously cheap prices.

'This guy's at the Ilford labs,' said Thomas, shuffling. 'I'll tell him to be careful.'

'Tell him to be very, *very* careful,' said Sergeant Nice.

When he got back to the police station, carrying the cine-camera, there was a message for him to ring Super Green. 'I'll make you a cup of tea while you do it,' said his wife sympathetically.

From the jovial play-acting tone in Super Green's voice, and from a certain hollow feeling in the telephone Sergeant Nice could tell that Chief Super Higginson was listening in on the extension. That and Higginson's stentorian smoker's breathing, which sounded on the phone like the beast from 20,000 fathoms.

'What, what, what's all this I hear?' asked Green, with bogus joviality. 'An outbreak of street thefts in your manor, Bainbridge?'

'Yes, sir,' said Sergeant Nice woodenly.

'Can't have this, you know. Graymouth's a family resort – must be kept safe for kiddies. Isn't that what you told the *Evening News?*'

'Yes, sir.'

'People will be stopping going to Graymouth if this goes on – regular crime wave, Bainbridge – getting like Chicago. People will be saying it's not safe to walk the streets in broad daylight. Cameras, bathing-costumes . . . not a nice experience having your bathing-costume stolen, Bainbridge – especially when it's wet.'

Higginson was trying to stop himself laughing; it sounded like the beast from 20,000 fathoms was starting to eat people.

'What are you doing about it, Bainbridge?'

'We're keeping our eyes open, sir.'

'What do you normally do – walk around with them shut? You want to watch that or you'll fall over the cliff into the sea.'

'Yes, sir.'

'What's your theory, Bainbridge? Or do the police admit themselves baffled? I thought I'd be reading in the paper that you'd called in the Yard by this time.'

'It's a sneak thief working round the clocktower. Snatching things while people are looking the other way.'

'He snatched anything today?'

'Yes, sir.'

'What?'

Sergeant Nice closed his eyes in dread. 'Six crash helmets and four pairs of motor-cycling gauntlets.'

'Say that again,' said Super, ominously. '*Six* crash helmets! Do you mean to tell me a sneak thief can make off in Graymouth carrying six brightly coloured crash helmets, in broad daylight, and not a single member of the local constabulary notice him?'

'He may have put them into something, sir,' Sergeant Nice said miserably.

'You mean – no, let me guess – in a bag marked SWAG or something?'

'No, sir.'

'And you haven't a clue – you *literally* haven't a clue?'

Sergeant Nice was very tempted to tell him about the cine-film then. But something could still go wrong: old film, fogged developing. Better to be prudent – he didn't want to be any more of a laughing-stock than he already was.

'Pull your bloody socks up, Bainbridge, or I'll have you shifted. That clocktower's in front of the police station, isn't it?'

When Green hung up, Higginson was laughing audibly. They both were. They'd have laughed on the other side of their faces, if they'd known what was to follow.

At five o'clock the next afternoon, young Thomas shouted and waved from his shop when Sergeant Nice was still the other side of Front Street. He was positively jumping up and down, like a chimpanzee before a tea party, causing passing holiday-makers to give him odd looks and his shop a wide berth.

He seized Sergeant Nice by his neatly starched shirt. The sergeant removed the sweaty hands with some distaste.

'C'mon, c'mon – I've got my projector set up in the back room – it's incredible – incredible. You won't believe it!'

From the look on Mrs Thomas's face, the chimp act had been going on for some time, and she obviously laid all the blame at the sergeant's door. Ignoring her ominous silence, Thomas bustled the sergeant into the back room, which was so dark that the sergeant walked straight into the projector, almost sending it crashing to the floor, and practically had to grope and crawl to a seat.

'All set!' yodelled Thomas. 'All *set*? Columbia Pictures present . . . the greatest mystery of all time . . . fit to stand with the sea drama of the *Mary Celeste* . . .'

The projector began to whirr. A perfectly focused picture of the clocktower bloomed on the screen, after the flashed sequence of numbers. It really couldn't have been clearer. There were the motorbikes; there were the bikers. The scene brightened momentarily, before the electronic exposure meter adjusted. A bright white glow coming from the right, lighting up the right-hand side of the bikers' faces.

'That's the street light exploding,' said young Thomas, needlessly.

The bikers' faces turned towards the light; looks of glee appeared on them. The bikers as a man ran off to the right and out of the picture. Other passers-by remained, motionless, looking at the invisible shower of sparks that lit up their faces. Nobody looking anywhere near the horse trough. Except the camera . . . Now for it! Now for a picture of the thief, good enough to give to every policeman in Oldcastle.

Nobody. Nobody. Nobody went near the horse trough.

The light from the right faded. The bikers began to drift back towards their bikes. One looked into the trough, saw his helmet was missing, began to gesticulate . . .

The reel of film ran out and the screen went blank, then dark.

'Run it through again,' said Sergeant Nice, letting out a long-held breath.

'I didn't spot it the first time either,' said young Thomas, smugly.

This time the sergeant watched the piled helmets in the horse trough. Their bulbous, shiny tops were quite visible over the rim. He ignored the departing figures of the bikers, kept his eyes so fixed on the helmets that he did not even blink.

'Stop!' said the sergeant. 'Run it back a bit. Now on again. Good God, I don't believe it! Run it through again.'

They ran it through ten times in all, while the sergeant chain-smoked four of the five cigarettes he allowed himself a day. Finally he said, and he was glad the room was in darkness,

'The helmets don't just vanish . . . they *sink*. Through the bottom of the trough . . .'

'Yeah,' said Thomas, breathily. 'They just sink. Did you see one of them suddenly roll clear of the rest?'

'Yes.'

'I've got it all worked out,' said Thomas, triumphantly. 'I've had time to think about it. That horse trough's a fake; it's got a false bottom. Did you know, there's an old manhole cover under there? I worked it out from the pattern of cobbles in the road. What a way to nick things! Everybody puts their bags in that trough. Distract people's attention, work the trap door and, bingo, you've got a new Japanese camera. Crafty sods, lurking down a manhole cover.'

'Let's go and have a look,' said Sergeant Nice, heavily. He knew there was something wrong with the whole theory.

They walked across and stared down into the sunlit depths of the horse trough. A woman was sitting on the far edge of the trough, with her bag inside, among the crisp bags and lolly-sticks. Sergeant Nice asked her to move it and herself; and for once he wasn't nice about it. He cleaned out the litter thoughtfully, as if he were recovering the Crown Jewels.

There was no crack or slit anywhere in the horse trough. Like most of its kind, it had been carved from one massive block of limestone. Sergeant Nice went over every inch of its surface, scraping away with his massive, many-bladed Swiss pocket-knife.

Nothing.

'That's mad!' exploded Thomas. 'There's *got* to be a trap door. We'll have to look from underneath – down the sewer.' People began to stare at him curiously. Sergeant Nice hauled him away by brute force, just in time.

They timed Operation Sewer for four a.m. Sergeant Nice had got a book out of the library which said that the flow of sewage was least then. It also mentioned choking concentrations of methane gas and the danger of being caught underground by a heavy rainstorm. Sergeant Nice did not mention this to Thomas, but he checked the midnight weather forecast; drought continuing.

They covered up the whole operation as a spot of night fishing; that would account for the old clothes and waders and possible smell on returning home. There was also the worry of Constable Hughes, covering the whole of Graymouth on his solitary Panda-duty. But Constable Hughes had been dealt with fairly thoroughly. Orders to keep his eyes open for a streaker on the golf-links up the coast.

'Any description?' asked Constable Hughes hungrily; he was a badly over-married man.

'About five-feet-eight, long blonde hair, aged about eighteen.'

'Female?' Constable Hughes' eyes positively bulged. It was like feeding candy to a baby.

'Old biddy who phoned in reckoned the young 'uns are holding orgies on the beach.'

No more trouble in that direction. Sergeant Nice still had his personal radio on the car seat beside him. Every time Hughes came on the air, he seemed a little further north.

'Right,' said Sergeant Nice, coming out of his professional doze at 3.45 precisely. They drove up St George's Road. Young Thomas leapt out, eager to try his newly invented patent hook for lifting manhole covers, as if he were taking part in the D-Day landings. By the time Nice had parked the car, he had lifted a square manhole set in the pavement that even an idiot could see was marked GPO.

The relevant manhole, as Sergeant Nice had feared, was right in the middle of the road. Even at four a.m., that was a bit nervous-making. They fished a clutter of red diversion signs and flashing beacons out of the boot. By the time they had finished, the diversion looked quite convincing. The beacons looked cosy, their beams exaggerating every stone in the tarmac.

The sewer lid lifted easily. Iron rungs descended out of sight. Sergeant Nice led; the rungs were slippery under his waders, but the smell wasn't too bad, only cloyingly human, like a bed that's been slept in too often. But the round manhole shaft was too narrow; not physically but mentally. Nice felt like a worm burrowing down through solid rock.

At the bottom, the heat of the sewage clamped round his waders up to the knee. There seemed to be stones lying on the bottom, half-bricks that turned treacherously under his feet. He stood clear of the ladder and switched on his rubber torch. A six-foot worm-hole of black brick stretched away on either side, glistening. Drops of warm bath-like water dripped off the roof on to his hair. The air was thick with smelly steam, like the Borneo jungle; he kept on wanting to hold his breath, breathe shallow. He made himself breathe deeply.

Which way? He had a sudden flush of panic. If he turned the wrong way, they could end up wandering through the maze that lay under Oldcastle. Fool! Sewers ran downhill to the sea.

Thomas arrived with a thumping splash that put drops on Sergeant Nice's face. He wiped them off carefully with a hanky; they left pale brown stains on the clean linen. 'You've taken your time!'

'Had to close the manhole quietly, didn't I?'

Closing it had been Thomas's own idea; Nice didn't like it. Suppose when they got back, somebody had parked a car on top? Suppose their torches gave out?

'Switch your light on,' he said savagely. 'Let's go. I don't want to write my memoirs down here.'

'Your what?'

'Scrub it!'

They seemed to wade on and on. Only two hundred yards, thought Sergeant Nice. In his youth, he had run that in twenty-two seconds. It didn't feel like it tonight. The black worm-hole went straight, without bend or curve. The sewage flowed forward at the same pace as they walked, so that the same patterns of oily iridescent scum and toilet paper, bobbing bottles and furred mounds of potato peelings kept pace with them, unvarying. As if they were walking on a treadmill staying for ever in the same place. Time had no meaning, space had no meaning in this bowel of the earth. Timelessness. Spacelessness. Warm water dripping on to them; warm sweat dripping off them. If they slipped and drowned, who would know? Someone would clear away the flashing beacons in the morning thinking them a joke . . . was this how methane poisoning felt, this strange other-worldliness? The book hadn't said what the symptoms were.

It was a relief to pass a side-channel, down which the sewage poured faster, breaking the surface of the scum. The smell here was horrific: sulphuric acid, man-hating; he supposed that in the main sewer, the scum kept the smell trapped, inside those great greasy bubbles that floated past like dead bloated animals. Mounds of khaki detergent-foam had built up round the side-inlet; they had to force their way through, up to their necks. The torch dimmed ghostly as it passed through the foam.

Still, they made progress. It was even comforting to meet a rat, up to its whiskers in scum, but swimming cheerfully and briskly, till its tiny eyes glowed red in the light of the torch and it fled away with frantic splashing. Good to meet something else alive.

Drip, drip, drip.

Suddenly Sergeant Nice knew quite positively that they would meet nothing human down here. Who would put up with this stench for all the Japanese cameras in the world?

The thought struck him like a bomb. Nothing human.

Something inhuman? That cared no more for the stench and heat and wetness than the rat?

Far ahead, in the swing of his torch-beam, the bottom of another ladder swam into view, like a pale skeleton furred with dried slime until its limbs were nearly as fat as a man's.

'We're here,' he announced roughly. Another round black worm-hole rose vertically above his head. He took a shallow breath and began to climb, rung by rung, stamping down his feet, making a hollow thrumming noise. What was he doing that for? To warn something? To frighten it, up there in the dark above?

It was a long climb up in pitch darkness. Front Street was on the cliff top, and the sewer would have run down to sea-level here, preparing to flow out into the harbour across the rocks. Sergeant Nice could feel every cubic ton of the wet sandstone cliff around him; dark, ageless, beyond the comprehension of man. Again that other-worldly feeling crept over him.

His head hit the underside of the manhole cover with a painful thud, so that he almost took his hands off the ladder to contain the pain. He clung to the metal rung with one hand and got out his torch with the other. He couldn't get the torch out fast enough. If there was anything to see, he would see it now.

Nothing. Or rather, a circle of black, featureless bricks, a rusty ladder and the rusty underside of the manhole cover. He swung the torch to and fro aimlessly. He tried lifting the cover; got his shoulders to it, neck bent, and heaved upwards till the iron ladder creaked and cracked warningly in its brick fastenings. Of course the manhole wouldn't move; it had several tons of limestone horse trough on top of it. He tapped it; it had no hollow ring. It *sounded* as if it had several tons of limestone on it.

Nothing; or exactly what anyone but Thomas would have expected. Not a sign of disturbance, not a crack or scrape in the brickwork. Sergeant Nice thought for a moment of his wife sleeping peacefully in the police station, across the cool fresh air of moonlit Front Street. Then, with a growl in his throat, he started down again. Forced young Thomas to climb up in turn and poke about.

'I want you satisfied. I don't want to bring you down here *again*.'

Thomas seemed to poke a long time, disconsolately; his figure, far above, outlined by a pool of torchlight at the end of a long black dwindling tunnel, remote as a star. Finally, he came clumping down.

'*Satisfied*?' It came out like a curse.

Thomas nodded, dumbly.

'Shall we look a bit further – down to the sea?'

'Yeah,' said Thomas defiantly. They waded on, very tired now. The sludge overtook them a little, objects left them behind and dwindled away into the dark beyond their torches. A dream of space and time and endless journeying. That was how it felt, an endless journeying through the black between the stars; lifetime after lifetime . . . Sergeant Nice shook his head angrily to clear it. Methane.

They came to where the old brick sewer became new concrete pipe, and a few bits of seaweed were stuck to the sewer wall. A sharp smell of the sea cut through the gaseous filth. They tapped on the sides of the concrete sewer and the concrete boomed like metal. They rejoiced, knowing that out there was the open air, and the waters of the harbour and the dawn.

'Seen enough?'

They turned back, suddenly eager to hurry, as if afraid their luck would run out before they reached the light. The sewer stream was against them now, kickable, rippling round their waders. Their wading broke the scum, the fat greasy bubbles burst and the smell of sulphuric acid tormented their lungs. Dark, cold, endlessly black without hope . . . Methane. Keep going. Methane.

Past one skeletal ladder. Finally, up to a second. Leaden legs, climbing it. For an awful second, the sewer lid refused to give. Then they were out, dumping paraphernalia in the car boot, and sitting in the car drinking coffee and watching for the coming of dawn, with their stinking waders lying outside like crumpled black corpses on the pavement.

They sat silent a long time. Then an early milk-float whirred and clinked past and broke the spell. Simultaneously they turned to each other and said,

'You bloody faked that reel of film, didn't you?'

Both their mouths dropped comically open. Both said, 'No – I thought *you* did.'

Their mutual amazement was too real to be a sham.

'Let's go and look at it again,' said Sergeant Nice.

There was no way the reel of film could have been faked. The movements of the motor bikers, of the by-standers, were smooth and unbroken. No sudden inexplicable jumps. The very slowness with which the helmets sank into the trough was unfakable. They watched over and over, ran it backwards, re-ran it, stopped it frame by frame. It made no difference. Frame by frame, the helmets sank; the top one of the pile tilted, fell and vanished in turn. They watched it so closely and so often, it became a meaningless sequence of coloured blurs, as if their eyes had burnt the emulsion off the celluloid. Finally, when Sergeant Nice could bear the dark, weary, claustrophobic tension no more, he switched off the projector and pulled back the lounge curtains. Full daylight outside; another lovely sunshiny day.

'It's insane,' he said. 'It just couldn't happen.'

'Oh, plenty of funny things happen,' said Thomas, off-hand but shifty, as if he were about to produce some dirty postcards.

'What do you mean?' snarled Sergeant Nice. The night had taken its toll; he had a splitting headache.

'Like people catching fire spontaneously and burning to a cinder, and the chair they were sitting in hardly scorched.'

'What the hell's that got to do with it?'

'Well – the world's full of unexplained things,' said Thomas, lamely. 'This magazine—' He held up a curiously purple publication, with the image of a fabulous sea-serpent on it and the title *The Unexplained.*

'You may have to sell that rubbish,' shouted Sergeant Nice, 'but you don't have to read it!'

'The world's full of doubting Thomases,' replied Thomas pettishly. Both of them were too angry, and too tired, to notice the pun. 'I think this horse trough's some kind of Mystic Portal or—'

'Mystic Portal my foot!' roared Sergeant Nice. 'Are you sure it's not a black hole, or a time-warp, or the Loch Ness Monster's arse hole?'

It was as well that the lounge door opened at that moment. Mrs Thomas thrust a head through, bristling with curlers. 'Well, if that's a night's fishing, it doesn't seem to have improved your tempers. Who's left those stinking wellies in the sink? And I'll remind you it's a quarter to seven and there's four bundles of newspapers on the front step waiting to be opened.'

Sergeant Nice left Thomas to his troubles.

It was no good starting with black holes. Better to start with Alderman G. G. Sharratt. Deceased, but at least real once. During his lunch break, Sergeant Nice drove to the newspaper office, where his mate the photographer, who owed him a few favours, showed him the back-editions for 1902, bound together in a faded pink volume nearly as thick as a coffin.

'Who you after now, Sarge? Jack the Ripper?'

Sergeant Nice's grunt sent him fleeing.

He picked up Alderman G. G. Sharratt very quickly. Opening a Charity Bazaar and Charades by the Sunday School, for the Relief of the Decayed Poor of Oldcastle. Ah, here he was again.

RELIEF OF EQUINE DISTRESS IN PRUDHOE STREET
FOR OUR FOUR-FOOTED FRIENDS

And there was a photograph of Giles Gilbert Sharratt; a thin, sad face under a formal top-hat, with deep Edwardian shadows round the eyes like a clown's make-up, and a drooping moustache over a drooping mouth. Not a villain's face; too sensitive. A source of relief to everything but himself. Laying his slender, pale hand possessively on his horse trough.

So much for Thomas's Mystic Portals. But the trough had begun life in Prudhoe Street. Right across town from Front Street.

He drove down there, and got lost. Prudhoe Street and the little Victorian terraces that had led off had been bulldozed flat. Progress had ordained a deserted three-lane by-pass, traffic islands where the long grass was reclaiming its own, and low boring factories in the distance. Only a few stumps of terrace remained on the fringes, with their long-gone neighbours' flowered wallpaper still hanging in wind-torn streamers from their newly exposed walls. Sergeant Nice sighed, and started knocking on doors. As he did so, his personal radio informed him that there had been a new theft at the clocktower. A bag of supermarket groceries. The damned stupid thing was growing insatiable . . .

He got no answer from the first four houses, though he had the feeling that people were at home; old people. The houses hadn't seen a lick of paint in years. Dirty lace curtains hung torn at open windows. Front gardens were long grass. A sense of hot hopelessness took hold of him. He'd try one more house. It looked more hopeful. Huge whitewashed seashells as well as flowers in the front garden; the gate tied shut with a loop of coarse white string; the knocker had been polished.

The half-glass door opened as soon as he knocked on it.

Was it an old lady standing there? Or a healthy, elderly, female tank? The flowered pinafore was stretched over a powerful bust and stomach. Arms like a stevedore's. The face was wrinkled, but the eyes were bright blue and bold.

'Come in, Sergeant, come in. When I saw you through the glass, I thought you were a military man.' It was obvious she approved of military men. He went in, wiping his shoes carefully, though the day was dry. He was a child again, arriving at his grandmother's.

'Cup of tea, Sergeant? I've just made a pot.' He gave in, sitting on an ancient but clean horse-hair settee, and listening to her putting on the kettle stealthily, behind a closed kitchen door. She returned, wiping her hands on her pinny.

'I'll let it stand and mash a minute. What can I do yer for?'

'Well, it's like this, Gran . . .'

Her eyes frosted. 'Don't you Gran me, young man. Me name's Sarah Trewhitt – Mrs Trewhitt to ye.' But there was a rough affection for all men in her voice that belied her look.

'I'm looking for a horse trough, Gra— Mrs Trewhitt. A horse trough given by Alderman G. G. Sharratt . . .'

'God love yer . . . that old thing. I mind the day it was dedicated. Eeh, we had many a good game in it, when we was bairns. It never done the horses much good, but we blessed it in the summer. Paper boats and plodgin' our feet in it. Poor Gilly Sharratt, he were a well-meaning man. Very fond of all sorts of science and progress.' She made them sound like minor male hobbies, like snooker or drinking. 'He did many a kindness, but folk never understood him. He put a gun to his head in 1926 . . . never married, you see.'

He looked at her sharply. But the tragedy of that death didn't touch her; she was back plodging in the glorious summer of 1903. Again that sense of strangeness struck him; the strangeness of time. She seemed like the horse trough, indestructible.

'What happened to the trough, Mrs Trewhitt?' Then he paused; she must be well over eighty. 'Perhaps you don't remember?'

''Course I remember. It was there till 1968, when they wasted the ratepayers' money building that great useless pass-by. Then the men came wi' a bulldozer – daft name for a thing – an' moved it.'

He sighed softly; that explained it. Between his seaside boyhood and his seaside manhood, the council had moved it to Front Street. He had a silly thought then – a little cold tremor of fear. A vision of the restless spirit of Gilly Sharratt, not understood, passionately addicted to science and progress. Still lingering round his horse trough and purloining modern examples of science and progress, like Japanese cameras. He remembered the sad face under the top-hat, the face that had put a gun to its head. They said the souls of suicides . . .

He shook himself; he was getting as bad as young Thomas and his bloody Mystic Portals. Afterwards, though, he would look back on the ghost of Gilly Sharratt with a sad longing; it was so much nicer than the truth.

'They've got it in Front Street now,' he said. 'The horse trough.'

She stared at him, wrinkling up her old face in incomprehension.

'They moved the trough to Front Street, Mrs Trewhitt.' She must be getting tired.

'Have they hell!' she said with great passion. 'Have they hell! I've got it in *my* back garden. Full of mulch for me rhubarb. I was so fond o' that thing that when they'd got it on the blade of their bulldozer, I asked them how much they would take for it. Give 'em a quid an' they tipped it straight over me back fence and laid it exactly where I wanted it – that's modern progress for you. And none o' the bosses any the wiser.'

He just gaped at her.

'Don't you believe me? D'you want to see it?'

She led him down her little garden, neat with rows of cabbage, lettuce and night-scented stock. And there it lay, shiny as a new pin, but full of a glutinous mixture of dark water, rotting lettuce leaves and what looked suspiciously like horse-manure.

'There's a poor old feller still comes by wi' a horse an' cart an' a few green vegetables . . . the horse is very obligin' . . . I nip out wi' a bucket an' shovel, soon as he's gone.'

'Two horse troughs,' said Sergeant Nice, thinking aloud.

'No! He never had two troughs, Gilly Sharratt. He wanted more, for the horses, but people just laughed at him. There was only ever one Sharratt horse trough, an' I've got it!'

'But, but . . .' said Sergeant Nice.

And then, in that neat sunny little garden, his mouth went dry with horror.

He had examined the horse trough in Front Street so often, he knew the pattern of fossils on it by heart. There was a place on the rim where the embedded fossils formed what looked like a twisted letter *H*, then a twisted letter *E. H. E. HE.* 'Hee, hee, hee, hee, hee' it had mocked him when his searches proved fruitless. Here was exactly the same pattern again, in exactly the same spot on the rim. What odds in the universe against the same thing happening twice, in exactly the same place? And the one piece of graffito the Front Street trough carried, scratched on its shining stone, the straggly initials *S.T.* It was here again. And he knew what the initials stood for . . .

'You scratched your initials on the trough, Mrs Trewhitt?'

'I did. Lucky I did, too 'cause somebody stole it, you know. For one night. I reported it to the police. But by the time they came next morning, it was back – I felt a right fool. Only when it came back it was empty. Somebody had stolen the mulch for me rhubarb. What some folks will do . . .'

The world reeled round Sergeant Nice in that neat little garden. What power in the universe could steal a horse trough that weighed several tons and perfectly replicate it? Am I going insane? he thought.

'Are you all right, Sergeant? That sun's very hot an' you've left off your cap. You've mevve caught a touch o' sun-stroke. You look like you've seen a ghost . . .'

Somehow he got himself back into the Panda. Its radio was burbling on about an RTA in Saville Street and requesting an ambulance; but it fed him like a fount of sanity.

There is a Buddhist saying that Sergeant Nice had copied out of a book. (He was fond of copying thoughts out of books.)

Even in the worst situation, there is usually some useful action that can be performed; if there is not, gather information; if there is no information that can be gathered, sleep.

He had not slept last night; not a wink. He had tried putting his head under the bedclothes, but the thoughts still came. Teleporting, Thomas's stupid magazine called it. Somebody had teleported the horse trough out of Mrs

Trewhitt's garden, made a perfect replica of it, and teleported two horse troughs back. Eight months ago, on the worst day of blizzard-chaos that Oldcastle had ever known. What power in the universe . . .? Something out of *Star Wars* . . .? And having performed this incredible miracle, they were using it for the purpose of petty theft. It was that contrast of utter power and utter pettiness that frightened Sergeant Nice.

The Russians? What would the Russians want with a wet bathing-costume? They could buy a Japanese camera anywhere, on the easiest possible HP terms!

That was it! They were *practising*! Practising for something much worse. It didn't matter if they failed in Graymouth. But suppose they set up something similar in Aldermaston or Farnborough, or the secret underwater weapons establishment at Portsmouth?

It was no good reporting this to the Supers. He needed . . . a scientist, of some sort. A scientist would understand; scientists had open minds . . . He reached for the phone.

'University of Oldcastle, Registrar's Office.' A female voice, cocky. A switchboard girl . . . not a scientist. 'Who do you want to speak to, please?'

'I'd . . . I'd like to speak to a scientist.'

'What *kind* of scientist? Which department? Biochemistry? Physics? Geomorphology? Materials Science?' She was taking the mickey; but Materials Science sounded right.

'Materials Science, please.'

'Ringing!'

It rang for a long, long time. Then another female voice answered, less promising and scientific even than the switchboard girl's.

'I'd like to speak to a scientist, please.'

'There's nobody here. It's the middle of the long vac.'

'Who're you, then?'

'I'm the cleaner.'

'Is there *nobody* about?'

'Mr Milburn was in last Thursday. But he's only a postgrad.' She made him sound nothing, as if she'd said 'postcard'.

'When will he be in again?'

'Probably Thursday. He has to see to things.'

'Is he on the phone?'

She was silent a long time, searching, then she gave him a number. He let it ring a long time, but nobody answered. He let it go on ringing, in a kind of sleepy paralysis, before he came to with a start and hung up.

Still, the mere idea of Mr Milburn gave him hope; perhaps he would listen, perhaps he would understand. But scientists required evidence as much as judges. He must, as the Buddhist gentleman said, gather information.

He had to admit he was a bit frightened of the horse trough now. He didn't know what other powers it might have. He was certainly convinced it could read his mind. Probably control his mind. It had made the two dogs fight and the woman faint. And that Brummy's car . . . So he approached the clocktower when it was thronged with gossipy holiday-makers. Leaned against it casually, as if his only concern was afternoon drunks and pickpockets.

It was easy enough to get a bit of the clocktower itself. There were places where corners of stones had cracked with decades of wind, rain and frost. He wriggled a loose piece of the stonework until it came off in his hand, warm from the sun, sharp-edged. He put it into his pocket, feeling like a vandal, suddenly blushing in case some holiday-maker was watching.

Nobody was watching; no holiday-maker, anyway. He eyed the horse trough warily. It looked genuine enough, as if it had been there for eighty years. But he was dealing with no ordinary clever-dick. It might be full of closed-circuit telly, radar, bugging devices. He sidled over to it; sat down cautiously on the edge.

The action sent a shiver up his spine, that at first he thought was nerves. But the pain in his buttocks soon convinced him otherwise. Under the afternoon sun, the trough was icy cold. The clocktower was warm, but the trough was icy cold. Got you, he thought, got you, you clever bastard. Clever, but not clever enough. First piece of hard evidence. Elated, he took out his Swiss knife. Mrs Trewhitt had carved her initials on her horse trough. He tried to scratch a mark on his.

It wouldn't scratch at all, even to the point where the knife blade broke and left him with a bloody, dripping finger.

People stared at him as he made his way casually home to get an elastoplast.

The sharp tap of metal on metal echoed up the dark length of Front Street. Sergeant Nice swore. There was no right time to do this. If he'd done it when the pubs were open and the juke boxes masked the noise, some amiable drunk would have ambled across to see what he was up to. The sounds of a man at work are irresistible. But now, in the one a.m. silence, the sound of hammer on cold chisel seemed as loud as the tolling of St George's bell.

He thought it would be easy. Two brisk taps and a piece of horse trough would be lying in his hand. Crinoidal limestone wasn't a hard stone; not like granite. But this trough . . . he'd already been at it for ten noisy minutes, hitting harder and harder so that blue sparks flew, like those from a cigarette lighter, briefly illuminating his large hands clenched tightly round hammer and chisel. And he hadn't even managed, as he saw when he shone his torch, to scratch the thing.

Suppose somebody came; suppose somebody saw him.

SENSELESS VANDALISM, SAYS MAGISTRATE
POLICE SERGEANT REMANDED FOR
PSYCHIATRIC REPORT

He glanced round again, scanning the street for any onlooker. He was getting more and more nervous. But he had to have evidence, material evidence, for Mr Milburn. It was pointless even to approach him without having something to show.

He stopped paying attention to what he was doing. The chisel slipped again on the cold stone, and the hammer nipped his finger. He threw hammer and chisel down in a rage, his eyes full of sweat. He had a sledge-hammer at home; never used for anything worse than knocking in posts at the Rotary Carnival. *That* would settle the bastard. He picked up the dropped tools and slipped away.

It was as well he did. As he closed his front door, headlights turning at the end of Front Street lit up the clocktower in every Gothic detail, bright and sharp as a new pin. Panda. Constable Hughes. Hughes getting out and flicking his torch briefly over the monument. Sergeant Nice switched on his personal radio and heard Hughes reporting in to Oldcastle Police Control.

'Ref telephone complaint in Front Street, nothing to report. No damage. No persons present.'

'Continue to visit at half-hourly intervals,' quacked an aggrieved female voice.

'Ten-four,' said Hughes in the forbidden American impersonation. The Panda oozed quietly away and turned left up the coast.

Hughes had given him half an hour. But somewhere in the darkened houses of Front Street an old biddy would be sitting by her window. Old biddies, in Sergeant Nice's experience, didn't seem to need any sleep at all. He was in for a long vigil.

At the end of two hours he came out at a smooth loping run, wearing plimsolls, black sweater and dark-grey flannels. It was hard to run at all, his legs were so stiff from being curled round a chair with tension. The hair was standing up on the backs of his arms, on his head; it was like the time they'd taken out that guerrilla camp in Borneo.

If anyone had seen him, they would have been scared. His Viking forebears had left him more than their broad shoulders, long arms and ginger hair. He struck the trough a terrible blow, up by its rim. It rang like a bell, but did not splinter. The hammer hurt his hands abominably.

A frenzy came on him; he hit again and again. *Boom, boom, boom.* Each time, the head of the sledge-hammer sent out a spray of vicious sparks, each time a little nearer to the actual clocktower. His sweaty grip was loosening. The last blow flew wild, bounced off the trough on to the clocktower itself. A great shower of stone hit him in the face, blinding him. He dropped the hammer, cleaned out his eyes and shone his torch.

A chunk had been smashed from the tower, where it adjoined the trough. A frighteningly large chunk, as if a shell had hit it. But on the trough itself, not a dent.

He thought wildly: This trough is impossible, impossible. There is nothing in this world so hard as this trough. Another, stronger wave of rage and hate took him. He began hitting harder, harder, harder. He no longer wanted a chip of it, for evidence. He wanted to destroy it, and those who had so insanely made it.

Harder and harder; part of him knew it would end in disaster, but the rest of him no longer cared. Harder and harder he hit, like a savage, a cave-man. *Something* had to give.

There was a sickening crunch. Something hard and cold and heavy grazed his face, flying through the air and landing yards away with a heavy, metallic clinking and rolling. He stood panting, blinded by sweat.

The hammer-haft in his hand was as light as a feather. He felt for the end. The head was gone; it was the head that had missed him by a fraction and landed down Front Street. He brushed the hair out of his eyes, words bubbling out of his dry, panting mouth.

'Oh dear, oh dear, oh dear!'

When he shone his torch, the trough was still without a scratch. He felt like crying.

Then, vaguely, he became aware that his torch wasn't the only source of illumination. Headlights had him fastened in a sharp glare. He saw the sign on top of the Panda.

'Hey, stay where you are! Don't you move an inch, my lad!' Hughes, getting out of the car.

It was all up; his life lay in ruins.

But Hughes' voice changed. 'Oh, it's you, Sarge. Did you get a glimpse of him?'

'No,' said Sergeant Nice, weakly. 'He was gone when I got here.'

'What's that you got there, Sarge?'

'Hammer handle. It's snapped off at the head.'

'Pity you picked it up . . . fingerprints.'

'Too rough.' Sergeant Nice showed him the old grey spelky wood of the handle. Suddenly, they were two policemen again, working in pursuit of an unknown criminal. 'The head must be lying somewhere. Look what he's done to the clocktower. A raving nutcase.'

'We'll never catch him now, Sarge. Funny the things people get up to. Wonder why he hated the thing so much.'

'I think we've given him a fright,' said Sergeant Nice. 'I doubt he'll be back.' He sighed regretfully. 'I was sitting up late, reading, and I heard the noise.'

'Old biddy who rang up reckoned it was loud enough to waken the dead.'

'I was sitting in the kitchen at the back,' said Sergeant Nice.

Sergeant Nice leaned his backside against young Thomas's shopfront and admired the sunset at the far end of Front Street. He had never enjoyed a week so much. All his life had been given back to him, and he savoured it like one returned from the grave. The smell of salt off the ocean, the sun on his bare arms, the lissome little bathing beauties, even the screaming children; all given back as a gift after that night of madness with the sledge-hammer. Oh, a story had gone back to the Supers, all right. The story of Sergeant Nice so lost in some old book that he couldn't hear a demolition in progress on his own doorstep . . . typical. Well, let them laugh. He could afford it.

The memory of the crazy Neanderthal man with the hammer had faded too. Soon, he would be able to think it never happened at all. And yet Neanderthal man had had his value. The thefts from the horse trough had stopped completely. Seven days now, and not a single complaint. Neanderthal man had broken something.

Or frightened something.

Anyway, there'd been no more funny business. The Supers said the thief must have moved on. They had fed a report of his modus operandi into the central crime computer, in case he tried other seaside towns. The Supers were satisfied; the crisis over. Perhaps, elsewhere, cameras and handbags and wet bathing-costumes were vanishing from innocent park benches or left-luggage lockers. But not on his patch, not in his manor. Sergeant Nice laughed to himself, softly. A passer-by gave him a funny look. Policemen on duty were not supposed to laugh.

Young Thomas came out of his shop, gave a sheepish grin that said all and began to push the shop's sun awning back into its overhead casing with a long pole. 'Peace an' quiet!'

'Peace an' quiet,' echoed Sergeant Nice.

'You'll have time to find my old cat, now.'

'He gone missing? Not like him.'

'Been gone six days.'

'Courting?'

'Not him. Neutered. Never known him miss a meal. Hope these vivisectionists haven't got him – or one of those fur gangs. They call those fur coats coney, but I swear half of them are cats. Cat from the Elite Fish-bar's missing an' all.' Thomas finished pushing his awning up, and paused, leaning on his pole. 'You know, it sounds childish, but I miss him. He used to come out with me while I did this – at the end of the day – and sit on the horse trough waiting for me to finish an' give him his supper . . .' There was a hint of a watery glint in Thomas's eyes.

'*Ye what?*' shouted Sergeant Nice.

'Feed him—'

'No – you said he used to sit on the horse trough. Waiting – when there weren't many people about.'

'Yeah?'

'The *horse trough.*'

Thomas said, 'Oh, Christ,' and they turned and looked at the horse trough together.

'No wonder it stopped nicking cameras and bathing-costumes.'

'I'd like to blow the bloody thing up!' said Thomas, vehemently. 'I was fond of that cat . . . what *is* it in there?' His voice rose and cracked in hysteria. 'Why the hell can't you do something about it? You're the police . . .'

'Got any suggestions? That won't land me in Morpeth for a month on a compulsory-treatment order?'

Thomas was silent.

Sergeant Nice said, 'You're round here all day. Do you ever get little kids playing in that horse trough?'

'No, no, never,' said Thomas. 'Never seen a little kid playing in it. Never in this world. Not without their mum watching anyway.'

He sounded very far from sure.

That night, Sergeant Nice had a dream. Normally, he never dreamt, or rather, try as he might, he could never remember his dreams. He remembered this one.

He dreamt he was lying in bed and the bedroom door opened and silver shapes came in. Shapes like silver men and women, with beautiful silver faces and huge, dark-blue eyes full of . . . nothing. They brought with them Thomas's black cat, and the striped cat from the Elite Fish-bar, and a little brown-and-white spaniel dog. They talked to the cats, which perched and slithered on their silver shoulders, in a cat language all prooks and chirrups. And the cats talked happily back. Sergeant Nice had never heard cats talk so much.

He dreamt that he raised himself up in bed, in his striped pyjamas, to greet them. But one of the silver women bent down and pushed back the bedroom carpet, to disclose a manhole cover in the bedroom floorboards. The cover was lifted; they descended, taking Sergeant Nice with them into a dim yellow light. And in the dim yellow light, huge glass bottles glistened. In the bottles floated dissected bodies of animals, like in the biology lab at school. From the necks of the bottles protruded not the usual corks, but the heads of Thomas's black tom-cat, the striped cat from the Elite Fish-bar, and the spaniel dog. And the heads were still alive; the tongues licked dry, open mouths in vain. And the heads were still attached to the glistening white entrails inside the bottles.

From the neck of the last bottle protruded the head of a little girl with long, blonde, greasy hair . . .

Sergeant Nice dreamt he turned on the silver people in a rage and shouted at their beautiful, vacant eyes. And the beautiful eyes cracked like glass, and from behind them green snakes slithered, slowly dripping down the silvery bodies. And then the bodies began to fall apart, like armour, and more green snakes dripped from every opening joint, until soon there was nothing but green snakes.

And Sergeant Nice awakened, sweating so much that his striped pyjamas were soaked. He went straight down to his office and checked the reports on missing dogs. There was a small brown-and-white spaniel reported missing, from the Esplanade Hotel. Answers to 'Midge'. Reward offered. Sergeant Nice sat at his desk till morning. His wife found him snoring, face down on his blotter.

After that, the sergeant dreamed his dream every night. At least the first part of it, the friendly part. But he would never return the chirruping greetings of the silver figures, no matter how earnestly they pleaded. For now he knew the truth about them, though he never again witnessed that truth. And each night the silver figures grew more frantically friendly.

By dawn, each morning, he would bitterly accept that he was awake for good; he who had slept like a top every night of his life. He would go downstairs and make a cup of tea, and then go to his office window and pull back the curtain and stare for hours at the horse trough in the first faint light of day.

The next fortnight became known in the Oldcastle force as 'the Clocktower Business'. Even the youngest constable never referred to it without tapping his forefinger to his forehead; even if the youngest constable had joined the force long after the Clocktower Business was over.

It began when Sergeant Nice gave out the day's duties the morning after he had first dreamed of the silver people. Constable Wayne would spend only half his time pacing the prom, admiring lovelies and making the yobs put their lollysticks in the waste bins provided. The rest of the time he would keep his eye on the area of the clocktower. Constable Broady would spend only half his time at the Haven, damping the ardour of the couples on the Haven Banks to a level acceptable to the eyes of mothers of families . . . Constable Hughes . . .

'But this bag-snatcher working near the clock,' said Constable Broady, 'he's not shown his hand for a week.'

'Then he's all the more likely to start again today,' snapped Sergeant Nice, in a voice that killed off any chance of reasonable argument. He looked pale and jumpy. It was not a time to argue. It was a time to wait, to have a word in the inspector's ear, when the chance arose. So they mulishly went off and did what they were told. 'Ours not to reason why; ours but to do and die,' as P.C. Hughes put it to his wife that night.

After the third fruitless day of clock-watching, they took to whistling the old music-hall song: *If you want to know the time, ask a policeman.*

Sergeant Nice's reasoning was quite sane, as far as it went. The Things in the horse trough were all too aware of what was going on around them. They could even sense what people were *thinking* round about them. While they knew the police were watching, they would do nothing. And the end of the holiday season was only a fortnight off. In a fortnight's time, the Things would be the inheritors of a dreary, empty, rainswept desolation, with half the shops closed for the season and never a skylarking child in sight.

By next season, having had their fill of tom-cats, They'd be gone.

*

The situation had seemed so nicely tied up. It tore apart in seconds. A motorcyclist, showing off, doing wheelies down Front Street at thirty miles an hour. A woman stepping out into the road, looking back over her shoulder to tell her husband she wouldn't be a minute. The biker missed her by inches, at some cost to his own skin. He came off spectacularly, the bike skidding along the tarmac throwing up showers of sparks and orange plastic from its winkers. The woman fainted. Her husband attacked the dazed biker and got roughed-up by the biker's watching mates. All four police were rapidly on the spot; all were kept thoroughly busy. They even had to call in assistance from the nearest Panda. Hughes controlled the traffic while Broady marked the position of the bike in chalk on the road. Wayne revived the woman, with advice from a crowd of helpers.

'Stand back, stand back, give her air!'

Sergeant Nice forced flailing husband and bikers apart with massive, patient hands. The Panda man sorted out the real witnesses from the false. Front Street was back to normal in ten minutes flat – a very neat bit of police work, if Sergeant Nice had to say it himself.

He was quite a long time realizing that something much more serious had happened, because the parents were trying so hard to be calm about it, so reasonable.

A child was missing; a little girl of five.

'It's so stupid,' the father apologized. 'She was there one minute, and then she just wasn't the next.' He didn't look frightened yet; just ashamed and angry at his own carelessness. 'She can't have got far . . . but I've looked all up and down Front Street. I can't think where she can have got to. I hope you don't mind us bothering you like this. It seems so silly. I mean, this is *England* . . .'

'When did you discover she was gone, sir?' asked Sergeant Nice. The terror in him made him speak slowly, ponderously.

Made him sound a real P.C. Plod.

'Just after that bike crash. We were all coming off the beach together, us and friends . . . we thought all the kids were together . . . they were all larking around in a mob. She was with her cousin Michael . . . she's not one to stray, ever. She's a timid little thing.'

The kids, when questioned, knew nothing. They had been too enthralled by the motorbike; and picking up bits of orange plastic for souvenirs.

Sergeant Nice glanced at his watch slyly, by the process of pretending to fold his arms. Fifteen minutes had gone by. That was a long time for a lost child. Usually the child came in first, bawling its head off, before the stupid parents had even noticed it was missing. He talked to his constables over his personal radio. Wayne working his way along the sea-front; Broady back in the Haven; Hughes working up and down Front Street, questioning people. Sergeant Nice was short and angry, anything but nice, barking down the microphone. The constables were squawking with indignation. What did he expect, miracles in a quarter of an hour? What the hell was the urgency; this wasn't Chicago! Was the father a millionaire or something?

After another hour had passed, the constables changed their tune. The beach was emptying; light starting to fade from the summer sky. The sergeant's wife made tea for the parents. The sergeant watched them sinking into some silent, horrible pit, from which they tried to escape by leaping to their feet, pacing up and down, or by sudden violent snarlings at each other. Only to fall back into their silent private pit again. The husband's hand sought the wife's blindly; the wife, as blindly, thrust it away.

When the child had been missing almost two hours, Sergeant Nice summoned assistance. Three more Pandas. He seemed to repeat the description over and over again: small and light, long blonde hair, wearing a pink dress. Had the child in his dream been wearing a pink dress? No, she had had no dress – no skin or flesh either. He closed his eyes, remembering the thing in the bottle – the thing that endlessly licked its dry lips.

'I'm going to look,' said the father. 'I don't want to criticize, but I know my own child better than—'

'Better to stay here, sir, with your wife. She could be found at any moment. We know what we're doing. We deal with a hundred lost kids a year, here. More lost kids than lost dogs. They always turn up.' But his words were hollow. Long blonde hair . . . timid . . . small and thin for her age.

Other people were helping to search now; deck-chair attendants, the girls from the lost children hut. Graymouth wasn't that big, and by this time the beaches and streets would be totally empty. Outside, it was dark. Sergeant Nice's wife came in silently and drew the curtains, as if to shut out the trouble.

The searchers were asking for torches.

His wife offered the parents more tea. They refused; then accepted, desperately.

I'll fix those bastards, thought Sergeant Nice. I'll fix those murdering silver bastards. If I'd fixed them before, this wouldn't have happened. It's my fault. I wanted everyone to be happy in Graymouth.

Even Them, he realized with bitter amazement.

But he'd fix Them now, if it was the last thing he did.

The call came through at nineteen-seventeen. Constable Wayne, his voice wild with relief.

'Got her. Curled up fast asleep, on a bench in a beach shelter.'

'Why the hell didn't you search there before?' Sergeant Nice's voice could not have sounded more empty of the gratitude he felt inside.

'I *saw* her before. But there was another family in the shelter with her, and I thought she was one of them. It was lucky I was passing just as they were going, leaving her behind. Talk about pig-ignorance! They've sat there with her all this time and never asked her where her parents were. They even gave her a butty . . . what kind of standards do these people have?'

Suddenly it was all over. The father began to swear and the mother began to cry. Sergeant Nice called up the police doctor, to come and give the child a once-over. The Panda pulled up at the door and the child was bundled in. He took a careful look at her, and decided she was nothing like the child in his dream.

The woman police doctor arrived, took mother and child aside into another room and returned, smiling. No crime. Now it was all fresh cups of tea and swapping of stories and happiness. All except for Sergeant Nice, watching and listening and writing his report at his desk, very far removed from all the fuss.

Finally, the father took Sergeant Nice's hand. 'Sorry to have troubled you. You've been marvellous. We were silly to have worried. Thank you, thank you very much.'

'No trouble, sir,' said Sergeant Nice.

He sat on a long time at his desk, when everyone had gone. Only the odd remark on his personal radio, from the solitary patrolling night constable, broke the neon-buzzing silence. That silence got bigger and bigger until it filled the room, until it filled Sergeant Nice's head.

He had had his warning. God had been very good to him. God had shown him what *could* happen; then taken all the agony away again.

But he knew he would not get a second warning. Reluctantly, he went upstairs and began to undress for bed.

Then he paused, sitting in his shirt and socks, the bedside lamp shining on his long, white, bony knees. He reached into the top drawer of his bedside cabinet, and pulled out an old, wrinkled address book he'd kept since his army days. He was very careful about such things; still kept in touch with a lot of old comrades. He turned the pages slowly; ran his finger down the column of addresses.

'Hurry up and get that light out,' grumbled his wife from the other twin bed. 'You're that restless these nights, I don't know what's got into you. It's not like you at all. I'm thinking of moving into the spare room, honestly I am.' She turned over with a great hump of protest.

Sergeant Nice made up his mind. Closed the book, *slap*. Switched off the bedroom light, *click*. And, having made up his mind, he slept as soundly as a log.

It was very easy, really; though it cost him two days' precious leave. The Supers grumbled about it still being the holiday season, but they had heard the first whispers about the Clocktower Business and thought it best to give him the break when he asked for it.

He made twenty phone calls before he went; drove nearly a thousand miles in his middle-aged Morris Marina. But at the end of it all, he had what he wanted. Ten pounds of plastic explosive. He gathered it cunningly, a pound at a time. Ex-sergeants of the Royal Engineers, who have mates still in the army, or working as quarry-managers, are never far from being able to lay their hands on explosive. The excuse he used was always the same; big old tree stumps to blow up in his new front garden. His old mates all made the same joke. 'It's lucky we know you, Bill. It's lucky you're not a Paddy. You *haven't* joined the IRA, have you?' And sound, sensible old Bill just smiled his slow, shy smile and let them get on with it. And got what he wanted.

He returned home; to a suspicious Mrs Bainbridge, who didn't quite accept this talk of old comrades' reunions. He spent a long and thoughtful time in electrical and model-aircraft shops. Then he rummaged deep into the old wooden cupboard that was the Graymouth police lost property store.

That night, his wife looked dourly at the large portable stereo radio-tape-recorder that lay in a thousand pieces on the kitchen table.

'That's not yours. That was handed in. That's stealing.'

'It was found on the beach at low tide. Soaked. It'll never work again. They wouldn't let me hand it in at Oldcastle . . . junk!'

'What d'you want it for, then?'

'That's my business.'

She swept off to bed in a huff. He worked on till the small hours, patient and sure, with his big square-ended fingers.

He stood on the cliffs at the end of Front Street, looking down at where shadows were slowly engulfing the hot golden sand and the last bathers. Few would have recognized him in his patched khaki slacks, garish beach-shirt and dark glasses. There was a camera slung round his neck; he looked a proper tripper. He was glad his wife had gone to the first autumn meeting of the Townswomen's Guild.

He held the portable stereo in one hand. It was exceedingly heavy; but then stereos were. It held enough! First, a tiny transistor-radio that at that moment was sending out disproportionately loud pop music. Second, two tiny radio-control receivers from model-aircraft, linked to two radio-control transmitters set up in the boxroom at home. Two of each for safety, in case one went wrong. He had always been a belt-and-braces man.

At the moment, the transmitters in the boxroom were switched on, the boxroom door was locked, and the only key was in his pocket. Because if his wife came home early and switched off those transmitters unthinkingly, the ten pounds of plastic in the stereo would explode, and the late Sergeant Nice would be spread in little gobbets of red flesh all round the roofs and gardens and telephone-wires of Front Street. They said the birds found them and ate them . . . there were worse ways to go. But while the transmitters went on transmitting, and the tiny receivers could receive their signal, the bomb was quite safe. For at least two hours, till the batteries ran out.

But if someone were to put the stereo into the bottom of the horse trough, and it vanished into oblivion, like the camera and the beach-bag and the wet bathing-costume . . . there would be one hell of a bang in oblivion. And that would be the end of oblivion and the poor suffering cats in the bottles, and the little brown-and-white spaniel, and the still-living remains of the girl with long, blonde, greasy hair. It would be a blessed release for her, thought Sergeant Nice. If she existed. If she didn't, it didn't matter anyway. Sergeant Nice giggled to himself. Then stopped; he didn't like giggling to himself.

There remained one problem. How to get the mice to take the cheese in the trap. He knew They knew They were being watched. He knew They could read the minds of people who came close to the clocktower. If he tried to plant the stereo himself, they'd read his mind and They wouldn't take the bait. The bait had to be put down by a third party, an innocent bystander.

That was the hell of it.

He looked up Front Street at the distant clocktower, nearly blotted out by the molten ball of the setting sun. Maybe They could reach out to read his mind even at this distance? Maybe they already had . . . Still, there was no harm in trying.

Not many people about. Only one kid, a thin kid of about

fifteen, laden with sea-fishing tackle, making his way home from fishing off the pier. Whistling, not a care in the world. The perfect innocent bystander. Only, he'd better *stay* innocent; if he ran off with the stereo, out of the range of the radio-control . . . But fishermen were usually honest, unlike yobbos. And this kid was too heavy-laden to run fast.

'Hey, mate!'

The kid stopped, mildly but instantly suspicious. Sergeant Nice almost wished he'd kept on his uniform and made out that the stereo was some new kind of radar speed-trap. But it was too late now.

'Do us a favour, mate?' Sergeant Nice cringed at his own forced bonhomie, real as a music-hall comedian's. 'You going past the clocktower, mate?'

The lad nodded, seeing no possible snag in that. He had a spotty face and was chewing gum. Sergeant Nice held out the stereo.

'Take this thing up to my wife, will you? She's waiting by the clocktower. I can't take photos with this great thing in me hand.'

The lad considered, seemed about to turn away. Sergeant Nice fished a fifty-penny piece out of his slacks. 'And buy yourself a drink for your trouble.'

That was a mistake. The youth's lip curled. The youth remembered practical jokes, of which he had suffered too many at school. He thought of *Candid Camera*. He thought about strange men who accosted you in the street.

Next second he was walking away. Sergeant Nice shouted after him in despair. The youth turned and gave him the two fingers of scorn.

Sergeant Nice went on waiting, trying to control himself. But he was pacing up and down, now, like a caged tiger or a man that needs the loo.

He almost didn't stop the Girl Guide in uniform. But he

was desperate. And didn't Guides still have something about a good deed for the day? She was obviously on her way to a Guide meeting.

He was more formal, this time. 'Excuse me, young lady. There's a lady waiting up there by the clock . . . she's my wife.' The child squinted her blue eyes against the setting sun. Then she nodded; she couldn't see if there was anyone there or not. 'Would you mind giving her this radio to keep for me? I can't take photos with it in my hand, and the light's already fading.'

The child considered a long moment, then nodded. Sergeant Nice gave her the stereo. She was a very small Guide, and her wrists were very thin. She had to use both hands to carry it, and then it was a struggle. She set off up Front Street, walking like a crab, but with her face aglow with her good deed and the setting sun.

Sergeant Nice held his breath till his lungs ached. She reached the clocktower, looked around, saw nobody there. She looked back enquiringly at the sergeant, her face a dark blank against the sun.

'Not there?' shouted Sergeant Nice. 'She must have gone to the loo. She'll be back in a minute. Put it inside the horse trough – it'll be safe there, till she comes back.'

The child was very still. Then she hoisted the stereo with great effort and, at the third try, balanced it on the edge of the trough.

'Lower it down *inside*,' shouted Sergeant Nice. 'It'll be safe there – for a minute.'

The child was very still again; doubtful about the wisdom of what she was being told. But she knew all about the apparent foolishness of adults. And the stereo was far too heavy to carry all the way back; and Guides were supposed to be obedient. With great care she lowered it down inside; her whole body pulled by the weight of it into a living horse-shoe stretched over the horse trough rim. The sergeant could imagine her tongue stuck out with the effort of it. Then she straightened up and waved. Sergeant Nice waved back and shouted,

'That's your good deed for the day.'

She waved again and ran off up Front Street, obviously late now for her Guide meeting.

Sergeant Nice waited and waited. The impulse to close in and look over the rim of the trough, to see if the stereo was gone, was unbelievably strong. It was a good job he had the patience of a fisherman himself. All the same, as if by a tidal drag, the horse trough pulled him nearer and nearer.

The sun sank finally in scarlet ruin of smoking clouds, behind St George's steeple. The dusk came purple and dim. And with it, what Sergeant Nice feared. Human voices at the far end of Front Street, drawing nearer. Dinner in the boarding houses was over. People were coming out for their evening stroll.

Two voices, one young and one older. Two figures, one small and one big. A woman and her child. The child's shrill voice carried clearly.

'But I *do* want a camera. If I give up my pocket-money between now and Christmas, and let you cancel my comics and—'

'I haven't got that kind of money, Susan. Thirty pounds for a camera . . . if only you'd saved up your pocket-money before your holiday like I told you . . .'

Suddenly, they were too near the clocktower, and Sergeant Nice was running, running to cut them off. If the child laid hands on that stereo . . .

He had to run past the clocktower, past the very rim of the horse trough to cut them off. As he ran past, it seemed to him that he saw a fleeting ghost of the stereo in the gloom. Glimmering, ephemeral and sunk halfway into the stonework. Then it was gone. He pulled up sharply at the sight, quite unable to believe his eyes, staring at the bottom of the horse trough, which was empty now even of dust and lolly-sticks, clean as the most thorough charlady could have swept it. He had never seen it so clean before.

'Stand back, madam!' he said. 'And keep that child well clear.' In spite of his ridiculous tourist-gear, the policeman in his voice made her back off quickly, to what might have passed for a safe distance. Even as an ex-sergeant of the REs, he couldn't be quite sure what damage ten pounds of plastic would do. Explosive was funny stuff.

There was the slightest tremor in the ground, as if somebody had dropped a big sack of potatoes on the pavement. A tiny piece of the rim of the horse trough fell to the road with a tinkle. Sergeant Nice picked it up; it was sharp-edged and cold, and fitted neatly into his hand. And that was all; except that as he looked at the fragment, it, and his hand, seemed to brighten slightly in the gloom.

'Ooh, Mummy, look. Look at the comet. Isn't it beautiful?' Mother and child were staring straight up at the sky, their faces lit with the same strange glow that had lit up the stone in his hand.

'It's not a comet, darling, it's only a shooting star.'

Sergeant Nice looked up too. A great streak of light fell down the sky, purple and green and white like a good rocket on November 5th. Except that it fell much more slowly, like slow-motion action in a Kung Fu movie.

'Isn't it *beautiful*,' repeated the child.

'I've never seen such a big one,' said the mother, grudgingly. Then she came out of her trance and turned to Sergeant Nice, expecting quite a different kind of explanation.

'I'm a police sergeant, madam. On observation duty. There's been a lot of bag-snatching round here, recently. I thought I saw somebody . . .'

'We've seen nobody,' she said, as if that settled it.

'Goodnight, madam.'

'Goodnight.' They moved on, resuming the argument about the camera.

Sergeant Nice stayed on, to watch the shooting star die down the sky, until every last fragment was gone. It took a long time to die; for a while it went on getting bigger and bigger. Something incredibly massive was burning out up there. He remembered, when he was a little lad, his granny had taken him out one night to watch for shooting stars.

'Every one you see,' she'd said, 'is a soul dying and winging its way to heaven.'

He'd known even then that they were only bits of space debris, hitting the earth's atmosphere at terrific speed and burning up. But he'd said nothing, because he loved his granny.

How many were there of You? he thought. You loving silver chirrupers with your rows of glass bottles?

Nobody would ever know now. Or where they'd come from, through the dark, endless years of space.

'You should have left us alone,' he muttered angrily. 'Graymouth's not your sort of place. It's a *family* resort.'

But they never came back to reply; not even in his dreams.